FOUR
Stories

By Philip Dampier

Copyright 2019 Stephen P. Dampier

Other Books by Philip Dampier

Robert H. and Tisza Books

The Red Shoe
The Old Man on the Mountain
The Third Witness
Collateral Damage
Can't Catch Me
Can't-Lose Her
Chasing Money

Shorter Works

Last Hunt
Hitchhiking, USA
The Five Wise Men

Religious Commentaries

To the Faithful Saints at Ephesus
Comments on Galatians
Comments on Verses from the Psalms

Table of Contents

A Faded Rose

Philip Dampier

Dedication

This story is dedicated to the love of my life for over 58 years. Grace Ann Peck Dampier has been my inspiration and my helper through good and bad, up and down. I love you, my Sweetheart.

CHAPTER ONE

The jangling alarm awakened Dawn Stevens with a jar. She was sure she had only been asleep for a few minutes. She had stayed up much later than usual the previous night holding on to Jim and not wanting him to go home. She dreaded this day, and now it was here. She wanted to give it a name. A name to remember it by. A name that wouldn't evoke sadness in and of itself. Dawn thought she would call it Bus Day.

Here it was, then, Bus Day had finally arrived.
She rolled out of bed and tossed her gown across the bedstead. A quick bath and then just enough time to get ready. Why did the bus have to leave so early? Who wanted to catch a bus at 6:00 in the morning? Who wanted to go to the square and tell someone goodbye at 6:00 in the morning. Dawn knew the answer to the last question because she didn't want to say goodbye at any time of the day. She spent the previous week crying but that had accomplished nothing but ruining the looks of her eyes and face.

A bath was followed by one hundred strokes of the hairbrush. Her hair was burnished auburn, and Jim thought it was beautiful, but sometimes she wished it was another color. She chose pink lipstick to accompany the light blush. She had a new dress from the big store in Orlando, and she planned on wearing it to the square. It was dark blue and very flattering, and she knew Jim would be pleased with how she looked.

3

She slipped on her black pumps and grabbed a small purse. She closed her door slowly and tipped toed down the hall and then the stairs. Elissa was waiting at the bottom of the stairs.

"My, my, don't you take the cake? That boy's gonna go crazy when he sees you and knows he leaving you here for all them other boys."

"There are no other boys, Elissa. You know that."

"But he don't, honey. Now you hurry back here, and I'll have your breakfast ready for you."

Dawn stepped across the wide veranda, down the steps, and onto the sidewalk. Ten paces up the walk and she could just make out the brown Army bus sitting adjacent to the town square. Several people were already there, and her heart skipped when she caught sight of Jim and his parents. It had to be a special day if Jim's dad came to town in the middle of the week. He usually did not leave the farm except for Saturday afternoon to get supplies and Sunday to take the family to church. He left church as soon as it was over, seldom taking time to visit or converse.

This day had been coming, in a way, since December 7th and the Japanese attack on Pearl Harbor. With the United States at war with both Japan and Germany and their allies, brown buses like the one in Farmville's square had appeared all over rural America. In the cities, trains were carrying recruits to the training facilities.

The only reason Jim had not enlisted earlier is that he wasn't old enough. It was now 1944 and a month earlier, January 8th, Jim had turned 18. Three weeks prior to Bus Day, Jim had told her the news. At first, she refused to believe it. They had plans, at least she had plans. The news produced the first real fight they had had during their time together. Jim was adamant. It was his duty he told her.

Jim looked over his mother's head and saw Dawn walking towards him. He swallowed a lump when he saw her all dressed up. She looked somewhat more beautiful than he had ever seen her. He spoke to his folks and then stepped out to greet her. He took her hand, and his face was one giant smile.

"Hi Dawn, I was afraid you wouldn't get up this early."

"Don't be silly. You know I wouldn't sleep in today. Hello Mr. and Mrs. Elwood. It's nice to see you."

"Hello, Dawn, it's good to see you, too. You look very pretty this morning," Mrs. Elwood said. "Isn't that a new frock?"

Dawn blushed. "Yes, Ma'am. My daddy got it for me on his last trip to Orlando."

The square filled up with young men and their families. An army sergeant was standing by the door of the bus, giving everyone a chance to say their goodbyes.

Jim took Dawn's hand and pulled her to one side. He was holding something in his left hand, but Dawn couldn't tell what it was because her eyes were glued to Jim's.

"I don't want you to worry about me, Dawn. When this is over, I'll be back, and we'll get married. In the meantime, I promise that I'll be true to you and I want you to be true to me."

"Oh, I will Jim. You know I will. I can't stand to see you go. I hate this darn war. I'm so scared something will happen to you."

"You just pray every night for me, and God will keep me safe. I'll be back for you, and that's for sure."

Jim pulled the rose up where Dawn could see it. "I brought this from our yard. I don't have a ring yet, so I want you to wear the rose to remember me."

When Jim pinned the red rose on her dress, he leaned in and whispered close to her ear. "Roses are the flowers of love, and this one is a sign that I love you and will always love you."

Dawn Stevens put both of her arms around her precious man and pulled him tight against her. She wanted to tell him how much she loved him, but she was so emotional that she couldn't speak. The tears were flowing down her cheeks and dripping onto the new blue print she had saved for this occasion.

Somehow his lips found hers, and he smothered any attempts she could have made to speak. They stood like that for a very long time, which later she would recount as less than a minute. She held the material of his shirt in her fingers in an attempt to prevent the embrace from ending.

The embrace and for all real purposes, her world, ended when the sergeant in charge called out "Alright you guys, let's get on board. The war won't wait."

Jim was one of eight boys boarding the bus from their county. Four, like Jim, were farm boys; the others came either from Farmville or one of the other smaller towns nearby. Most all of them graduated the summer before and had spent the time waiting for their names to appear on the draft board roll. Rumor was that America would soon be invading Europe and more and more troops would be needed. June 6th, 1944 was just over three months away.

Dawn stood immobile, watching the smoky exhaust from the old diesel bus rise into the early morning air. There was a slight wind, but the cold she felt was more than the wind chill of the post-dawn temperature. She finally turned and headed up the street to her house. She wished she'd worn a little sweater or at least put a shawl around her shoulders. The chill she felt would not have been put off by a wrap, however.

Her house was on the main street of town, just a few blocks from the bank her father owned and ran. It was a large two-story house, but only a part was used by her and her daddy. She stood at the edge of the walkway and looked at the house. It was white with dark green trim, but the paint was aging, and here and there pieces were flaking off. If her mother were still alive it wouldn't look like this; she would never have allowed it. The roof, like all the others on Magnolia Street, was composed of black shingles but due to the war in Europe, new shingles were hard to find.

The town of Farmville served as the center for area barn tobacco and watermelon farmers. The war had not increased the need for watermelons, but tobacco was in high demand. Every farmer that could get a tobacco allotment had planted every inch of it in tobacco. One thing soldiers seem to have in common besides guns was cigarettes. The problem was, however, the war had taken all the laborers from the watermelon and tobacco fields.

Dawn put one foot in front of the other and eventually made it to the front porch. She cast a glance at the geraniums in the two large pots by the double doors. The pink ones had been her mother's favorites, and she couldn't get through the door without seeing them and thinking of her. Today was different. All she saw was wilting flowers in faded pots. Her vision was filled with the view of the rear end of a brown bus that was passing through small towns in Florida on its way to Camp Blanding.

Dawn opened the door and closed it quietly behind her. She heard noises in the kitchen and knew that Elissa was fixing breakfast. Even the thought of Elissa's wagon wheel biscuits and fried eggs could not shake her depressed state.

"Is dat you, honea?"

"Yes, Elissa. It's me."

"You see yo're man off?"

"Yes."

"You okay, sweetheart?"

"No. No, I'm not."

Elissa appeared in the hallway, her salt, and pepper hair tied up in a bright peach colored cloth. She was wiping her hands on her long white apron as she approached Dawn.

"Now, now, now," she said as she reached Dawn and pulled her to her.

"Don't you worry, now child, God's got this thang. Ever thangs gonna be alright, just you wait and see."

"What's wrong here?" a large voice boomed out from the staircase. "Are you crying, Baby?"

Elissa let Dawn go and turned to the large man at the bottom of the stairs. Her eyes spoke one message to him and then her voice another.

"Jim left for Blanding this morning, Mistur Stevens. On the army bus. Dawn seen him off."

"Oh."

Daddy Stevens moved quickly across the floor. Much faster than you would think a large man could move. Even before Mrs. Stevens has passed away, Dawn occupied the center of his life. Had it not been for his wife, he would have spoiled her beyond hope. He gathered her up in his ample arms and hugged her.

"It will be just fine, Dawn. He'll be back soon, don't you worry none. We got those Germans on the run. It'll probably be over 'fore Jim ever gets to the war.

"Let's have some breakfast," he stated to the world, "I'm starved.

"Dawn, what's that flower you're wearing?"

"It's a rose, Daddy. Jim gave it to me to remember him by, and I'm not hungry. If you'll excuse me please, I'm going to my room and get ready for school. I still have two months before I graduate."

Before Daddy Stevens could answer, Dawn ran up the stairs to her bedroom on the back corner of the house. Her

9

windows opened to their backyard which was filled with flower beds and beautiful shrubbery. She threw back the drapes and stared out the window. In her mind, she was seeing the bus moving from town to town. She did not think about the young men going on board at each stop but instead tried to visualize what Jim might be doing and thinking.

She had plenty of time to finish her preparations for school as she had gone to see Jim off looking her very best. Dawn pulled herself away from the window and sat briefly at her vanity. Her hair had already been brushed to an auburn sheen, but she gave it a couple of pull-throughs for good measure.

She had just the slightest blush which she left and touched up her bright pink lipstick. It was a habit. Right at that moment in her life, she had little interest in attracting anyone's attention, especially boys. She had hers, and she didn't want another one. She had sworn to be true to Jim, and she intended to do it.

Dawn stopped by the kitchen to kiss her daddy and tell him goodbye. She would no more think of leaving without kissing him than she would consider going to the moon or New York City.

"I'll be a little late tonight, Baby," her daddy said. "Got a meeting with the directors. Ellisa'll have supper for you, and I'll be home before you know it."

"Yes, Sir. I'll be doing my homework I suppose. Daddy, how long do you think it will be before Jim can send me a letter?"

"Well now, Baby. He's going to be mighty busy for a while I'd think. The mail's not too fast these days either, what with the war and all. Don't expect too much, okay?"

Dawn stood still for a minute. She tried not to let the disappointment show on her face. She hadn't thought about Jim being busy. Too busy to write her. She planned on writing him at school and mailing it afterward. She expected he would be just as eager to write her. What if they shipped him off before he had a chance to write? That would be terrible. She fought back a tear. She couldn't fall apart with every new obstacle; she just couldn't.

Dawn walked down her own walkway to the public sidewalk and made her way down the street to a large rambling old house covered in ivy and half hidden in azaleas and crape myrtles. Two medium-size dogwoods guarded the front porch, and the swing hung on the far end.

The swing was occupied by Dawn's best friend, Charlotte Weber. The Weber's were old residents of Farmville, dating back to the turn of the century. Mr. Weber, Charlotte's father, ran the big mercantile store in the center of town.

Charlotte stood up when Dawn started up the steps. Her eyes were wide when she saw Dawn's new dress. New dresses were very rare in Farmville.

"Dawn, when did you get that new dress?"

"When Daddy went to Orlando last month."

"Why haven't I seen it?"

"I was keeping it a secret to wear when Jim left. The bus with our boys left early this morning."

"Dad says a lot of things are getting hard to find now. I usually get a dress when something doesn't sell in the store. Now, with the rationing going on dresses are hard to find."

That was one thing about the war that evened a lot of folks out. No matter how rich you were, you got the same ration stamps as everyone else. Course if you were really rich you could buy things on the black market, but in a town like Farmville, it would be greatly frowned on. The citizens of the town and county prided themselves on their patriotism and someone dealing in the black market would be socially ostracized if it were known.

Dawn didn't say anything in response to Charlotte's comment, her face taking on a far-away look.

"Oh. Are you alright, sweetheart?" asked Charlotte.

"Yes. No. I don't know. I'm scared Jim'll get hurt or even killed. I couldn't stand it if that happened."

"I'll pray for him. We can pray for all the boys who left today. I bet our homeroom teacher will let the class pray for them as well. The preacher will have the whole church pray come Sunday."

The two girls turned and started their walk to the high school with Charlotte doing her best to cheer Dawn up. It was a tough job because Dawn's mind had traveled back in history to when she was in the eighth grade. That was the year she had first noticed Jim. It was also the first year Jim had noticed her. He had been in her grade for seven previous years, but they had seldom spoken. He was a farm boy, and that meant he rode a school bus. She walked to school, and the other walkers were her friends. The students who lived on farms were seldom if ever in town and so even though she knew him and he knew her, they were nothing more than schoolmates. Until the spring of 1940 that is.

CHAPTER TWO

Perhaps it was because during that school year she had changed from a skinny girl to one with curves and shape. She had nice clothes, and her mother had taught her how to dress. She always looked neat, and she was a good student. Perhaps it was because during the same period Jim began to mature himself. Though awkward at times, he was growing taller, and his work on the farm had filled his arm and leg muscles out.

In American history, their seats were side by side. Dawn found herself sneaking looks at him, and often she caught him looking at her. When she caught him, it made her blush. She wondered if he was thinking what she was thinking. She, like most eighth graders who lived in town, knew little about sex. Those who came from surrounding farms had somewhat of a better idea because they had been exposed to the beginning of new life with various animals on the farm. What she had in mind was nothing like reproduction. It was a dream that he would take her in her arms and put his lips on hers.

She had never been kissed, of course. It just wasn't done much when you were fourteen; at least not in Farmville. At least she didn't know any girl who admitted it. But, there was no rule against thinking about it. And so she glanced at Jim and made up her own stories of what might happen if they were together.

And then on the last Saturday of April, something did happen. The new movie, "Pinocchio," made it to the movie theater in Farmville. The Star Cinema was only open on Friday nights and Saturdays. The first showing was right after lunch on Saturday, and this particular movie brought a crowd of young people. The bike rack in front of the building was filled with both boys' and girls' bikes.

Charlotte and Dawn walked to the Star as they called it, together, only to find a line outside the ticket window when they arrived. They were prepared to move to the line's end when they heard a voice. It was Jim, who was in the middle of the line.

"Hey, Dawn, I saved your place just like you asked me to."

Dawn blushed at his words and then saw Jim's friendly wave. He was smiling at her, and everyone was looking at her and Charlotte. Embarrassed, the two girls moved up the line and squeezed in just in front of Jim.

"I didn't ask," Dawn whispered.

"I know," he whispered back, "but I was hoping to see you here and..."

She blushed again. "Thanks, we'll get better seats."

"I was hoping the two of you would sit with Blair and me."

For the first time, Dawn noticed Blair, another student from her class. He was already talking to Charlotte. Charlotte wasn't blushing, Dawn noticed. Why was she blushing? She suddenly felt warm all over. What she had dreamed about was happening, and she didn't know what to do about it. The line moved, and they were closer to getting inside where the movie would start, and she could just sit and not have to talk.

"Sounds good to me," Charlotte said. "Can Dawn and I sit next to each other?"

Both boys grinned and nodded. Dawn was glad she didn't have to talk. Everyone paid for their own tickets, and then each of them got popcorn and a fountain drink. Dawn bought a Seven-Up so that if it spilled, it wouldn't discolor her blouse. Both girls were wearing white blouses and plaid blue A-line skirts. Nearly every girl entering the theater had discolored saddle oxfords and white socks. They were definitely the 'in' thing.

Several of the boys in the movie line were wearing shorts and cotton button up shirts, but Jim and Blair were wearing blue denim overalls, and long sleeve shirts with the sleeves rolled up. They looked like they had just come from chores on their farms which was the truth. Both boys had slicked their hair down with a dab of something, but Jim's dark black hair seemed to have a mind of its own. The tanned skin of the boys' faces and arms were in stark contrast to the fairer skin of the two girls.

Charlotte's hair was coppery red, and her nose was covered in freckles. Her nose was short and turned up, and her smile was a foot wide. She had beautiful teeth, and she liked showing them. Dawn's hair was just auburn and shorter than Charlotte's. Dawn's skin was untanned but had a naturally darker color as if her ancestors were from a southern European country. Her face was without blemish, and since she was too young for makeup, it had a fresh, clean look about it. Both girls were pretty in their own way, and the two boys were well aware of their charms.

The foursome made their way down the aisle, the boys allowing the girls to pick where they would sit. Charlotte picked a row about mid-way down and stepped aside so that Blair could go in first. She followed him in and stopped at the third seat, Dawn behind her. Jim paused until Dawn was in her seat and then turned to sit down himself. He held his drink in his left hand and put the bag of popcorn between his legs leaving his right arm free. Dawn watched, wondering if he had done that on purpose. His arm landed on the slim divider between the seats and sort of dangled off the end. She was holding her popcorn in her left hand and was keeping the greasy bag up off of her skirt. She thought, *what if he wants to hold my hand? What should I do?* She didn't know. She wanted him to do it but what would Charlotte say? What if some of their friends came by?

Jim glanced at her and grinned before putting his hand in his own bag of popcorn. At that moment the lights dimmed way down, and the coming attractions began. Suddenly, Dawn saw Jim's arm change position and then his hand move towards her. She panicked. He gently took the popcorn out of her hand and then moving it towards him, held it up for her to use. This allowed her to move her drink to her left hand and eat the popcorn with her right. She tried to be careful, but twice her left arm brushed against his right. Each time small shocks went through her body, and she felt a warmth in her neck and face. She was glad the lights were down, and she kept her eyes focused on the screen. She didn't dare look at him. She didn't look at Charlotte either.

She was making a dent in her popcorn when the cartoons flashed on the screen; the theater became much lighter. She glanced at Jim, and the realization came to her that his bag was still between his legs and he had not eaten any more from it. She felt that warmth in her neck again as she thought about what that meant. She had an idea. Instead of reaching in her bag she took hold of it and moved it towards him. He looked at her with a question on his face. She gave the bag a short shake and mouthed, "You next." Jim smiled and took some of her corn then took the bag back. Back and forth they went, eating from the same bag and occasionally taking a drink of their sodas. It necessitated a certain amount of face turning, and even in the dim light, she could see the satisfaction on his face.

When her bag was empty, they switched to his and before they knew it the second cartoon was over and neither had seen much of either one. The cartoons were followed by a newsreel, and they were caught up in the war scenes for a few minutes. A travelogue followed, and then the main feature came on. The theater was quiet for a change, even though it was filled with teenagers. The popcorn was gone, and so were the sodas. Jim's arm was back on the armrest poised as before.

Dawn didn't look at it or at him but stared at the screen. She told herself it was important to do that. She stole a glance at Charlotte and saw that her hands were folded in her lap. Dawn decided to do the same thing. She tried to stay as close to the middle of her seat as she could. Jim was obviously as far towards her as he could get.

Her heart wanted her to move her hand next to his and see what would happen. No, she was sure what would happen. She wanted it to happen, but she didn't. She was confused. Her mother had told her about forward girls and how you could get a bad reputation by being easy. She didn't want to be easy, whatever that was, but she wanted Jim to hold her hand. She tried to concentrate on the movie, laughing at the funny parts and being frightened in other places. Twice she almost looked at Jim, but she knew she shouldn't do it.

Twice her left hand started to move from her lap towards the space between her leg and his. What was she doing? She jerked it back and felt the flush again.

Dawn wanted the movie to be over. She had thought it would be fun to sit with Jim, but now she knew it wasn't. She couldn't enjoy being with Charlotte, and she couldn't enjoy the movie. All she could think about was his right hand and her left. She wanted them to touch, but she didn't dare. What would Charlotte say? What would her mother say? More than that, what would her daddy say?

And then it was over, and the lights came on. The theater was not large, but it seemed as if every teenager in Farmville was there. Everyone in town would know she sat with Jim. Did she care? Her daddy was a banker, and Jim was a farm boy. She was dressed like a banker's daughter, and he was dressed like a farmer. She thought she should be embarrassed, but she wasn't. A stubborn streak hit her then and there. Not unusual for Dawn, she could be very headstrong when she put her mind to it. She looked up at Jim and smiled. Instead of following him out, she walked right beside him.

"What did you think of the movie?" she asked.

"It was good. This was the first time I watched a movie with a girl."

She had not expected that and it caught her off guard. She found herself blushing again. When would she stop that?

"How was it? I mean with a girl?"

"Nice. You're very pretty."

"Thank you and thank you for helping me with the popcorn. That was a little awkward. Did I eat too much of the corn?"

"No," he laughed, "I should have gone and got us some more, but I didn't want to leave."

By this time they had reached the exit, and the crowd spilled out on the sidewalk and street. Several of her female classmates called her name. She knew it was their way of letting her know they had seen her with Jim. The foursome reached the bike rack where the boys had left their bicycles. Jim spoke first.

"Can we walk you to your houses?"

Charlotte answered first, "That would be nice, thank you. We live close by."

The boys retrieved their bikes, and the four of them started up the sidewalk towards the residential area of Main Street. Charlotte and Blair were in front and Dawn, and Jim followed. Jim had fooled with his bike for a minute to give his friend and Charlotte a head start. Dawn wasn't sure if it was to give the other couple space or to give she and Jim space. Either way, she was happy.

They walked quietly away from the noise of the theater crowd, neither speaking, both seemingly in deep thought. Dawn was having trouble with her emotions. Her feet were barely touching the walkway, and she felt like she was in a dream. She ventured a slight glance at Jim and found he was looking right at her. There was the warmth spreading from her neck and coursing through her body again.

"I heard you have a nice house," Jim said.

"It's okay. I don't think much about it."

"I live on a farm."

"I know."

"Our barn is bigger than our house."

"Really. I don't know much about barns, I guess."

"Would you like to see it sometime?"

"Oh, that would be nice. How far from town do you live?"

"About six miles; up the Alachua road for five and then on a dirt road for another."

"And you ride your bike?"

"Faster than walking."

"Yes, I guess so." This brought forth a smile, and it was if the ice was finally cracked. They kept chattering until suddenly they were at Dawn's home. Jim nodded as if affirming the information he had received about her house.

"Wow, your house is big. Almost as big as our barn. Your yard is big too."

"We have a flower garden in the back. Would you like to see it?"

Jim paused and then shook his head. "I'd like to, but I've got to get home. I've got lots of chores to do before dark. See you Monday at school."

"Sure."

"Thanks, Dawn."

"For what?"

Now it was Jim's time to blush.

"For sitting with me and letting me walk you home. I enjoyed it."

"Me too."

Jim smiled and then got on his bike and rode up the street to where Blair was waiting. The two of them spun around and pedaled rapidly past Dawn on their way to the Alachua Road. Both boys waved as they sped past.

Dawn watched them disappear into the town's traffic and was startled when Charlotte spoke to her.

"Well, Miss Dawn, you got yourself a beau."

"One time at a movie doesn't mean he's my beau and what about you and Blair?"

"I don't know. He's a farm boy, and I don't think his family has much."

"Charlotte, that's awful. What's his family got to do with him?"

"Well, if I have a boyfriend I want him to be able to pay for things for me."

"Sure. But in the first place, you can't have a boyfriend because you're too young and your folks won't allow you to date."

"Neither will yours. I'm not saying a word about Blair or what happened today and you better not either."

CHAPTER THREE

Mr. Stevens was in his office reading the paper and Elissa was busy fixing Saturday night's supper. Dawn was in her room, lying on her bed, trying to understand her feelings. They were new and strong and scary. Mrs. Stevens was in the living room sitting in the big flowered chair next to the front window. She had been sitting in that same seat when Dawn and Jim had appeared on the sidewalk.

Dawn was a pretty girl, and Mrs. Stevens had been expecting a boy to show up sooner or later, but she was hoping for later. She had not mentioned that she had seen the two of them when Dawn came in. She was just thankful that Theodore had been busy elsewhere in the house. He could be difficult where Dawn was concerned. He would fight her growing up without even realizing it. Best he not know about today's events.

Inez Stevens sighed and pushed herself out of the large chair. She was not feeling good lately, and it seemed as if just getting out of a chair created a problem. She was so glad to have Elissa's help with the housework and cooking. Elissa moved around the house with such little ado that one hardly knew she was there. Inez didn't want to climb the stairs again but she knew it was the only way to talk to Dawn in private and she very much needed their talk to be private.

Inez stopped outside her daughter's room and knocked softly on her door. She didn't feel she had to knock, but it was one of the ways she had taught Dawn to observe the privacy of others.

"Who is it?"

"It's your mother."

"Oh, just a minute."

There were the sounds of scurrying around, of a drawer closing, and then the door was pulled open.

"Hello, Mother. What are you doing upstairs?"

"I wanted to have a little chat with you, dear. I'll just take a seat in this comfy rocker that belonged to Grandmother Stevens."

Dawn moved to the edge of her bed and sat down, her legs crossed underneath her. She had transitioned from the movie outfit to an everyday dress. As usual, her room was neat, and things were put away in their proper place. Inez wondered what had been put away before the door was opened. She moved it to the back of her mind in order to bring the reason for her unusual climb up the stairs before bedtime to the forefront.

"I'm interested in knowing who the young lad was standing outside earlier. The one with the bicycle and overalls."

"His name is Jim. He's in my class at school."

"I see. And why was he outside our house, may I inquire?"

"He and Blair walked Charlotte and me home from the movies. Wasn't that nice of them?"

"Perhaps. Did you arrange to meet them at the theater?"

"No, Mother. They actually were there ahead of us."

"Did you sit with this Jim during the movie?"

"Yes, Ma'am," she said with eyes averted and head down.

"I see. Whose idea was that?"

"They asked us."

"And you said, yes?"

"Yes, Ma'am, we did."

"I see. Did this boy touch you?"

"No, Ma'am. He's a gentleman."

"I see. Did you hold hands?"

There was a pause in Dawn's answer. Not a long one but to a discerning mother it was long enough.

"I see."

"Did we do something wrong, Mother?"

"Dawn, sweet child, I am more concerned about what you wanted to do rather than what you did."

"But, Mother..."

"You're only fourteen, Dawn. Too young for getting involved with a boy."

"I'm not involved with Jim. We're just...just friends; that's all."

"I'll not mention this to your father, Dawn. Keep yourself away from this boy and any other that comes around. And, they will come around. You are a very nice looking girl, and boys will soon find that out. I want you to be pure when you get married. Do you understand me?"

Dawn wasn't sure she exactly understood, but she thought she had a good idea. Her mother had never spoken a word to her about being pure and what that meant but girls at school were saying things, and she was struggling believing what she heard much less understanding it all.

"Yes, Ma'am. I understand. You don't have to worry, Mother. Jim and I are just friends. That's all."

Dawn and Charlotte met in the parking lot of the First Baptist Church Sunday morning before their youth class. They joined arms and whispered all the way across the lot and into the building.

"Your mother called my mother," Charlotte said.

"I'm sorry. She was in the living room and saw us out the window. She thought the worse, I think."

"My mom was sure we were up to no good. I had to talk for thirty minutes to convince her we weren't *doing* anything. What's with grown-ups anyway?"

"They're afraid we won't be pure."

"Well, I'm lily white pure, I think," Charlotte said.

"Did you hold Blair's hand?"

"No, and he didn't hold mind. I saw you sharing your popcorn with Jim, though. How did you keep from touching his hand?"

"I was careful, but his hand did brush mine a time or two."

Charlotte's eyes widened. "How did it feel?"

"I felt hot and scared. It made me nervous."

"I would have died!"

The conversation was brought to a sudden halt as the two girls reached their Sunday School room. The looks the other young people gave them left no doubt as to the conversation that had been going on before their arrival. Dawn was so glad that Jim went to a small church in the country and was not there. She intended to ignore looks and comments and did so as she and Charlotte took their seats.

After the worship services were concluded, the whispered conversation resumed out the door and into the parking lot. Several teens walked by and tried to start a discussion but were rudely ignored. The girls had decided on their defense, and its main tenet was silence. They planned on meeting in the afternoon for a walk downtown in the small park just off Main Street. It had sidewalks with flowers, and here and there green benches sat alongside the paths. It was important to have a strategy for school the next day.

When Dawn returned home from the walk, she got a glass of sweet tea from the icebox and carried it upstairs to her room. She closed the door and turned the small skeleton key to secure it. She opened the bottom drawer of her dresser and lifted the stored blouses up revealing a small notebook. She extracted the book, replaced the clothing carefully and moved to the vanity which also served as her desk. Pencils lay next to the lamp, and she picked one up and placed the lead in a small handheld sharpener. The shavings fell into the small trash can by her chair.

When the pencil had a nice sharp point, she opened the book to her last entry and began to read her previous notes before starting anew.

Dear Diary, Today is the most exciting day of my life. The cutest boy in my class asked me to sit by him at the movies. We saw Pinocchio, but I'm not sure I remember it all. Every time Jim looked at me I felt goosebumps on my arms, and hot flashes went through me. It was so... I'm sorry I don't have a word for it. I'm still tingling inside. I know he wanted to hold my hand and Dear Diary, I wanted him to, but I didn't let on. I was too scared. Just feeling his hand brush my arm was all I could handle. I had to keep my eyes on the screen because I wanted to look at him and I knew if I did he would look at me and I would be in trouble. Is it possible for a person to just melt? He held my popcorn for me. Wasn't that nice? After the movie, he walked me back to my house. It was just like I was on a real date only, you know, I'm too young to date.

Dawn's mind and heart were trying hard to get together. She had to close her eyes and make herself focus. So much was going on inside her that she didn't understand and there was no one to talk to about it. Her mother had already closed that door, and she didn't dare open one with her daddy. That would be a disaster. He would probably foreclose on Jim's parent's farm, and they would move away.

Dear Diary, Yesterday, just as I finished writing to you, Mother came up to my room. She saw me talking to Jim. She must have x-ray vision because I think she knew what I was feeling. I don't know how she could do that since I didn't know myself. She told me I couldn't go to the movies with Jim because she wanted me to be pure when I got married. What if I married Jim? I'm not sure if I know what pure means. I've heard about "Sweet sixteen and never been kissed," but Jim and I didn't even hold hands. That's a long ways from kissing, I think. Now, Diary, the big question is what am I going to say to Jim at school? Should I act like nothing ever happened? What if he asked me if I like him? What if he wants to sit by me at the movies next Saturday? Oh, Diary, what am I going to do?

Monday follows Sunday every week, and sure enough, when Dawn woke up the next morning it was Monday, and school started at eight. She vacillated between being excited and dreading the whole thing. She took extra time picking out what she would wear and then putting it on. She almost broke the brush in her hair trying to get it to shine. She looked at her face in the mirror to make sure there were no spots or blemishes. If only her mother would let her use just a little lipstick or rouge.

Dawn stopped by Charlotte's and retrieved her off the front porch swing. They each had a small paper sack which contained their meager lunch. They could have had a bag full, but they were conscious of their waist size and were not taking any chances at calories. Along the way, other girls joined them. The boys mostly rode bikes and sped by the girls so that they could get to the playground and toss a baseball around. A lively chatter sprung up and much to Dawn's relief nothing was said about Saturday. That waited until the first class.

Dawn's first class in the morning was English. Her seat was on the far side of the room in what was designated the first row. Jim's seat was against the other wall which was the fifth row. She was near the front, and he was in the back. She was opening her textbook when Jim walked into the room. He turned his head towards her and smiled. She felt a nudge in the back. The girl behind her whispered just a little too loud.

"There's your boyfriend, Dawn."

Dawn turned red, and Jim winked at her. Dawn turned to the grinning girl behind her and between gritted teeth hissed, "Shut up, Gretchen, you're just jealous." That was met with laughter. Dawn buried her head in her book. Why had she said that? She never talked that way. She liked Gretchen, and sometimes they studied together. Mrs. Anderson came in from the hall and closed the door to the room. It was instantly quiet, except for snickers from two boys in the rear of the class.

"Excuse me, Robert and David. Please see me after class."

She looked at Gretchen and then at Dawn. She didn't need to speak; the look was enough. Dawn pretended to be deep in the English textbook and Gretchen was looking for something in her small purse. When Mrs. Anderson turned to write on the board, Dawn made a hasty note from a small piece of scratch paper and carefully folded it.

When the bell rang, the class stood up and began filing out the door. Dawn turned around and held her hand out to

31

Gretchen. Gretchen opened her hand and the hastily created note dropped into her palm. She didn't open it but put it in the pocket of her dress. She walked past Dawn and out the door. Dawn stood still until the last student had exited and then she moved quickly to the hall and her next class. She was glad to see that Jim was nowhere in sight.

Lunch came and went. She silently prayed that Jim would not come sit with her. She was already as embarrassed as she could be. She would have to sit next to him in American history, and that would be difficult now, she thought. Charlotte and two other friends sat with her, and she was glad to see that Blair was at a table with Jim and several other boys. Things were normal, and that was good.

American history came the second period after lunch. Jim was in his seat when she walked in. He never took his eyes off of her as she crossed the room. He had that same slight grin that she was becoming used to. She sat her books on the desk and sat down. Jim leaned over and spoke, his words barely audible.

"I wish I was your boyfriend."

Dawn stared into her history book. She was afraid to speak. What if someone heard him?

CHAPTER FOUR

Saturday afternoon came again. There was a Johnny Mack Brown movie, and Dawn knew every boy in the county would be there. Jim would be there. He had told her Friday that he would save her a seat on the same row as before. She had decided earlier in the week that she would stay home that Saturday and visit with her mother. Inez was feeling worse and had not been moving around the house much. It was a good excuse.

After lunch, Charlotte knocked at the front door. She was dressed for the movies, maybe a little overdressed.

"Come on, Dawn, we're going to miss the show."

Dawn shook her head. "I'm not going, Charlotte, I'm going to stay here."

"Oh, Dawn, please. I need you to be with me. Otherwise, it won't work. You know that."

"I'm not sure it's a good idea."

A booming voice filled the room. "What's going on, Baby?"

"She won't go to the movies with me, Mr. Stevens. Make her go."

"Of course she's going. You go have fun, Baby, I'll sit with your mother. Go, go. Here's a quarter, have popcorn on me. Ha, ha, ha."

Dawn took a deep sigh.

"Let me change my blouse; I don't want cola or popcorn on this one."

In a few minutes, the girls were at the theater buying tickets. There were plenty of girls for a western they noticed, especially older ones. Drink and popcorn in hand they headed down the aisle to where they had sat the previous week. Sure enough, two empty seats were available between Jim and Blair. Both boys were in overalls and shirts just like the week before, and just like they usually wore to school. The trailers were already running, and the girls got settled as quickly as possible. Jim held Dawn's popcorn, and after she sat down, he placed it between them as the week before.

Dawn saw Jim set his cup down in the aisle leaving both hands free. He was now able to hold the bag in one hand and get popcorn with the other. It also increased the chances that Dawn's hand might touch his. To be honest, this was not lost on Dawn. In spite of her mother's warnings, she secretly hoped Jim would be bold enough to take her hand. She had decided that if he did she would not protest too much. The trick as she saw it was how to make that possible without it seeming that she did. It had to be him not her, but she knew she had to make it feasible for him to do it without him feeling awkward.

While the fistfights and gunfights were taking place on stage, a minor drama (depending on your point of view) was happening in the fifth row back on the left-hand side of the middle bank of seats. Dawn raised her left hand just above Jim's right hand which was holding the bag. She deftly retrieved a few kernels of corn, and as she withdrew her hand, it rested on top of Jim's, but only for a few seconds. He glanced from the screen to her, but she was looking straight ahead as if nothing had happened. When she finished the corn, she let her left hand drop down beside her. It was on the seat not her lap. She waited. Suddenly the popcorn bag moved from Jim's right hand to his left. The left arm rested on the dividing armrest. It stayed there for several minutes. Dawn though the movie would end and it would still be there.

Jim was not looking at her, and he was not looking at her hand, he was looking at Johnnie Mack Brown. He seemed totally engrossed in the hard riding scene racing across the screen. The music was quite loud and the screen alternated between bright and fading light. Dawn realized she was not breathing. It was like Christmas morning all over again when she held the big package from her parents but wasn't allowed to open it until the Brownie was used. The word was suspense. Suspense and hope and just a little dread. What if he just sat there? She would feel like a fool, and she would know at the same time that the magic wasn't on both sides of the seat divider.

The screen darkened, and the music rose to an almost deafening pitch. Her eyes were on the screen too, and the music made her tense. Then she felt his hand. It gently, almost without pressure rested on hers. She flinched and almost moved her hand. No, she did move her hand but not much. He closed his over hers. Her heart beat so loud that she was sure Charlotte heard it. She glanced at Charlotte, but Charlotte was looking at Blair. She looked at her hand, the left one, the one Jim was grasping. His hand was rough, and she remembered he worked on a farm. She didn't mind the roughness. She didn't mind much of anything. Then she looked at Jim. He was letting her see the small grin that she was beginning to love. She felt herself smiling back. She did smile. She turned back to the screen. She started to pull her hand away, but he held it too tightly. He turned her hand over and put his fingers out. Without thinking about it, she spread her fingers and clasped his hand.

It was done. She had committed. Did it mean she was now impure? What if her mother found out? Her daddy? The other kids. Then the defiant streak arose again unbidden. She liked holding Jim's hand. She liked everything about Jim, and she didn't care who knew it. Well, maybe not her mother just yet.

School ended near the end of May. The last day Jim asked Dawn to walk to the school bus with him. There was no handholding on campus, but they walked side by side and pretended. When they got to the bus, Jim stopped and looked at Dawn who looked right back.

"We're harvesting watermelons next week. Would you like to come out and watch one morning?"

"I don't know. I'm not sure my mother would approve."

"My mom said she would come get you and bring you home. She wants to meet you, Dawn. You can help by bringing water into the field to my dad and me and the other workers."

"I'll ask. I'd like to come, but I'm not sure about my folks."

A week later Dawn came home from visiting Charlotte to find a pick-up truck parked in front of her house. She wondered who it could be. She hoped it wasn't trouble of some kind. Dawn opened the front door and walked into the hallway. There in the living room was her mother sitting in the flowered chair and across from her was a younger woman with dark black hair. Her back was to Dawn, but Dawn could tell it was Jim's mom. What could she possibly be doing talking to her mother? Dawn almost got past the door when her mother called out to her.

"Dawn, would you join us, please?"

Dawn answered, though her voice was just above a whisper. She moved on trembling legs into the immaculate room and stood where she could see her mother and the visitor's faces.

"Dawn, this is Mrs. Elwood. She's your friend's mother."

"It's nice to meet you, Mrs. Elwood," Dawn managed.

"I've heard a lot about you, Dawn. You're as pretty as I was told."

Dawn blushed and then found herself unable to speak. Finally, she got a weak, "Thank You" out.

"Dawn," her mother said.

"Yes, mother."

"Mrs. Elwood has invited us to her farm. She thinks you should learn about watermelon farming. What do you think of that?"

Dawn could not believe her ears. Was her mother actually entertaining the idea of their going? She had not dared hope

37

such a thing. Mrs. Elwood must be very convincing. What would her daddy say, that was the next thing.

"I think it would be fun. I hear it's hard work though. Jim told me it really gets hot in the field."

"Yes, that is true, but Janice tells me there are some big shade trees along the edge of the field and her husband has put a chair or two there. While you watch the watermelon business, Janice and I are going to look at her quilts."

Janice Elwood smiled at Dawn. It was a kind of knowing smile, Dawn thought. Dawn instantly liked her.

"I offered to come get you in the morning, but your mother says that your father will be glad to drive you out to the farm and come get you after lunch. What do you think of that?"

"Daddy's going to take us out to the farm?"

"Yes, of course. I haven't told him yet, but he's off, and he's got very little to do."

The trio chatted for a few more minutes before Dawn asked to be excused. She had to run back over to Charlotte's and tell her the wonderful news.

Saturday morning started warm and grew warmer. Dawn and her mother arrived just after 7:00. The men were already in the field and so Mrs. Elwood drove Dawn across the farm to where the watermelons were growing. Dawn got out by the chairs and stood to look down the rows of watermelons. Jim and three other men were spaced out, each one between two rows of melons.

In front of them were Jim's father and an older black man. The two of them had sharp curved knives in their hands and were bending over the melons. One and then the other would cut a melon from the vine and turn it over so that its white-yellow rind would show.

Jim was between the two inside rows, and when he came to a cut melon, he would pick it up and hand it to the man on his left. Then the melon would pass across the rows to the edge of that section where it would be sat on the edge. Each man, in turn, would pass their melons and so for each step through the field four melons would move to the turn-row as it was called.

Under the tree was a large number 3 washtub with a hunk of ice in it. The ice was floating in the water. Next to the washtub was a metal pail with a matching dipper. After about 30 minutes Jim stood erect and waved at her. He pointed to the tub and made a motion of drinking. Dawn took the dipper and put cold water in the pail. She then took the dipper and pail and walked down the row that Jim was on until she reached the place where they were.

All the workers stopped, wiping the sweat off their faces and gathered around the pail for a drink. Jim introduced Dawn to everyone. He couldn't stop grinning at her, but she was now used to it.

"What d'ya think?" he asked.

"It looks like hot and dirty work to me. You do this all day?"

"Yep. All day and every day but Sunday for two weeks or so."

"These are really big melons. They look heavy."

"They're Black Diamonds, and they weigh between 40 and 50 pounds. Worth about a penny a pound. Over there," Jim pointed across the current field to another patch of melons, "are the Charleston Grays. They only weigh about 30 to 35 pounds. Not as sweet as the Diamonds though."

An hour later the scene was repeated. Each time Jim would tell her something about harvesting and selling the melons. She could tell that it was very important to him and she couldn't help but think all she knew about watermelons before that day was how good they tasted cold on a hot afternoon.

Noon came, and everyone walked out of the field and up to where Dawn sat. Soon they were all in Mr. Elwood's truck. Dawn sat up front with Mr. Elwood, and the others climbed in the back of the truck. The floor of the large bed truck was several inches deep in straw. The five men found a spot and lay down. By the time they reached the Elwood's farmhouse all five of them were asleep.

Mr. Elwood said very little to Dawn but did manage to thank her for toting the water. He offered her a full-time job for the next week if she wanted it. Of course, she wanted it. She wanted anything that would put her near Jim Elwood. All she needed was for her mother to convince her daddy.

Chapter Five

One long week passed before Jim's first letter came. Dawn did not receive the envelope until she got home from school. Dawn read it and then reread it as often as she could find the opportunity. She, of course, had written him every day including the day he left on the bus. The letter was not long, and the letter itself contained the reason.

Dearest Dawn,

   I got here safe and sound. We've been running ever since. By the end of the day, all us guys fall in our bunks and don't move until revelry at 4:30 A.M. I thought I was in pretty good shape after football and basketball, but they are running us ragged.

I sure do miss you and can't wait to see you again, and I can't do that for eight more weeks. I got two letters from you already, and it sure was good to hear from you. I would have written sooner but we just now got paper and pens and permission to send mail. I wrote to you and Ma. Dad won't miss me until watermelon picking time.

Don't forget what I told you about the rose. If you want to date other boys, I'll understand, but I hope you won't 'cause I love you very much.
Love,
Your Jim

"Dawn, would you please pass the black-eyed peas?"

Dawn's daddy asked. "Dawn... Dawn. Where is your mind child?"

"I'm sorry, Daddy. What did you want?"

"The peas, Dawn. Please pass the peas. Why are you so distant today?"

"I got a letter from Jim today. It was my first one, and it wasn't very long."

"What did he say? I'm sure he's very busy."

"Yes, he is, but it's not fair that they don't give them time to write."

"I'm sure once he's done with basic training he'll have more time to write you. You really care for him don't you?"

"Yes, I love him, Daddy and I plan on marrying him as soon as he comes back home."

"I see. You're young to be making that kind of a decision, I would think."

"I'm almost as old as Mother was when she married you and I've known Jim since first grade. We've been best friends since the eighth grade. That's a long time, and we each know the other very well. He loves me, and I love him so why shouldn't we get married?"

"This is a bad war, Dawn. We are losing a lot of boys. What if Jim doesn't come back home?"

Dawn's fork stopped halfway to her mouth. For an instant, she was frozen. She couldn't move or think. The moment passed, and she was able to speak. The strain in her face was echoed in her voice.

"He has to come home. I can't live without him and I won't."

"That's nonsense. Thousands are getting the word about their loved ones, and life goes on. It has to; otherwise, we would fail to exist as a people. Your mother died, and the two of us are still here. It was hard but we are still here and will continue to be here, and we will carry on living our lives because that is how we survive as a people."

Dawn sat quietly, her fork back on the table. Hardly a day went by that she did not miss her mother. Because she had had Jim, it made the pain of losing her mother easier to bear. She had not thought about the grief her father bore every day. Her parents had married in their late teens, and she had not been born for ten years afterward. Her mother had often told her that she had given up hope of having a child and then one day there was Dawn, born in concert with the rising sun of a beautiful day.

The passing of Dawn's mother was similar in nature. The day before she had been in the hospital but that afternoon they released her. She had come home and immediately went to her room and to bed. It was obvious that she was ill, but the hospital had not known what to do with her and so had sent her home to die in her own bed. Dawn and her daddy were in the room with her. Dawn's daddy sat in a large chair not far from the bed, watching his wife of 37 years. Dawn was sitting in a small straight chair next to the bed holding her mother's hand. She was not aware of her daddy or his thoughts. She was too engrossed in her own sense of loss to think about what this might mean to her daddy.

The last real conversation that had taken place between Dawn and her Mother had been several days previous. Her mother sat up in bed propped by several large pillows, a tray with a glass of sweet tea on it sat in her lap. Dawn was sitting in the same straight back chair listening to her mother talk.

"My days are few, Dawn and I want you to promise me something."'

"What is it, Mother? You know I will do anything for you."

"I want you to promise me you will look after your Father. He knows all about banking but little else. You will need to run the house and see that things are taken care of."

"I will. I'll take care of things. I'll help Daddy all I can."

"I know you are crazy about that Elwood boy, but I don't want you to be so involved that you forget to take care of your Father. Do you understand me?"

"Yes, ma'am. I love Daddy very much, but I think I love Jim with all my heart. If he asks me to, I will marry him as soon as I graduate."

"That's another thing. I won't be here to see you graduate, but I want you to know how proud of you I am. You are a smart girl and a caring girl. Don't let your feelings for Jim cloud your thinking. There are other things a young girl can do besides get married right out of high school."

"I know what I want, Mother, and its Jim Elwood."

In spite of what her mother said, Dawn did not really believe that her mother would die that soon. Sometime during the last night her mother was alive, she fell asleep in the chair by her mother's side. Unbeknown to her, her daddy had picked her up and lay her on the couch opposite the double bed. He then took her seat in the straight back chair and held his wife's hand. He could feel the pulse grow weaker as the long hours of the night stretched away.

The sun came up just after 5:00, it's pink and orange rays casting light and shadows into the main bedroom. At 6:00 Mrs. Stevens passed away, her husband still holding her hand, his eyes red from lack of sleep but mostly from the tears he had shed.

Dawn was still sleeping, and her daddy left her that way. He undressed his wife and washed her body. He dressed her in her favorite dress. Her eyes were closed, and her hands crossed on her waist, looking for all the world like she was taking an afternoon nap. Mr. Stevens washed his own hands and face and went into the kitchen to tell Elissa. He wanted her to be there when he woke Dawn up.

Jim's letters came on a fairly regular basis. Usually, Dawn received a letter every other day. He wrote mostly about his daily activities as he and his company progressed through basic training. He evidently was learning a lot about Camp Blanding itself. He frequently wrote about how large it was and how many miles they hiked from one part to another.

Reports were being circulated that the camp was as large as the fourth largest city in the state and its hospital was one of the largest in the state. Jim seemed proud to be a part of the largest training center in the USA, and so he wrote a lot about the camp itself. Although Dawn asked questions about him and where he might be going, he avoided much in the way of personal information.

The weeks dragged by, punctuated by the arrival of the postman. Graduation came. Jim would not graduate, and Dawn's mother would not be present. What should have been a very happy day in Dawn's life turned into more frustration than fun. The graduates had a small party after the ceremony and Charlotte and Blair were there together. Charlotte tried to be Dawn's friend, but it was difficult with Blair holding to her. Charlotte promised to come over the next day, and the two of them would take a bike ride to the small lake on the Eastern side of town.

The graduation that Dawn was most looking forward to was to be held at Camp Blanding the last day of May. It was scheduled for the Saturday after her high school one. Dawn's daddy had promised to drive her, Charlotte, and Blair over for the ceremonies. Every day the excitement built up. Dawn spent hours talking to Charlotte trying to decide just what she would wear and how she would fix her hair. Dawn could not keep her excitement down, and she seemed to fill every room with happiness when she walked into it.

Thursday she walked into her house and made her way upstairs. In her hand was the thickest letter she had received from Jim and she wanted to be in private when she opened it. She was sure it would contain information about the graduation and his leave after it. She was hoping he would have enough leave for them to get married. Once in her room, she shut the door from Elissa's prying eyes and ears and sat down on the white chenille bedspread and slowly unstuck the flap.

The letter was written on a lined pad, and Jim's letters were steady and clear. She was always surprised at his neat handwriting. Most boys, in her opinion, had terrible handwriting. The letter began with an update on the previous day's activities with occasional comments on how he missed her and wished she was there to see all that was going on. She smiled as she read through the first two paragraphs, feeling his closeness, just knowing that the words were his gave her a warm feeling.

Then she started the third paragraph.

Dawn, I'm afraid I have some very bad news. Our graduation exercise has been canceled. We have been given orders to ship out tomorrow for -----------. By the time you get this message, I will be gone from Camp Blanding. I am so sorry that I will miss seeing you and being unable to tell you goodbye. This is so sudden, and it makes it a little scary. I guess something happened to change the plans. We don't get any news, so maybe you know more about it than I do. I will write you and let you know where I am as soon as I am able.
I love you more than ever and can't wait to take you in my arms again.

The letter went on for another paragraph with sentimental words and thoughts, but they were lost on Dawn. One part of the letter stood out in her mind. She knew it was not good news, but she wasn't sure why. What was happening in the war? She had been working on her finals for school and thinking about Jim, and the news was, well it just was. She didn't know what. Jim was leaving ahead of schedule

47

with no graduation and no leave. That was frightening, and it had to mean he was headed to where the fighting was.

Dawn put the paper back in the envelope and rushed down the stairs and out across the veranda. She made it to Charlotte's front door in record time, and when it opened, she quickly stepped inside. Charlotte and her mother were standing just inside the door.

"What in the world is wrong, Dawn? You're out of breath," Charlotte's mom said.

Dawn was clutching Jim's letter in her hand. She waved it at Charlotte and then burst into tears. Sobs wracked her body and Charlotte grabbed her and moved her to a cushioned chair. She held on to her hand and talked softly to her. Charlotte's mother headed for the box of tissues, great concern on her face.

"What is it, Dawn? What's wrong? Did something happen to Jim?" Charlotte asked.

"Here, Dear, wipe your eyes and let's talk about it, okay." Charlotte's mom said.

Several minutes passed, and the three of them stayed as they were, Donna slumped in the chair, Charlotte's mom holding a box of tissues while Charlotte continued to hold Dawn's hand and whisper in her ear.

Dawn sat up, shook the letter and then exclaimed, "It's Jim. They've canceled the graduation and liberty. They have left the camp. He tried to tell me where they went, but it was blocked out. He's headed for the war; I just know he is. I can't stand it."

Both mother and daughter set in to calm their neighbor and friend. Both of them wrapped their arms around Dawn and held her tight. It was what a girl who's lost her mother needed. Soon they went into the kitchen for a cold drink and some fresh baked cookies. By supper time Dawn had regained control, at least temporary, of her emotions.

She read the third paragraph to Elissa before her daddy came down for supper. Elissa made a great to-do and tried in her way to comfort her. It helped, but the pain was still there. Mr. Stevens was more jovial than usual, as the bank was making good progress in spite of the war. He was surprised to see his previously excited daughter sitting at the table looking quite remorse.

"What's wrong, Baby? You look sad tonight. Tell daddy what's going on," he said.

"Jim's gone. The whole company is gone. They left this morning, I guess."

"Where's he gone to, Honey? They move him to another training site?"

"I don't know. The army blocked out the place so you can't read it. It must be over there where the war is."

"Hmm, well there has been talk of our opening another front to help the Russians out, but that seems to be just talk at this point," Mr. Stevens said.

"They left without graduating and with no leave at all. Why so secretive about where they are going if it's not to war?"

"I tell you what. In the morning I will make a few phone calls. In the meantime, I have a little surprise for you."

"What is it?"

"After supper. We'll eat our supper and then I will show you my surprise."

Elissa cleared the dishes, and while Dawn played with a slice of apple pie, her daddy lit his pipe. He smoked Prince Albert tobacco, and he liked to have a pipe after his evening meal. The aroma was pleasant and held a sense of comfort to Dawn. She pushed the pie aside and said, "I'm ready to see my surprise. Is it in the living room?"

"No, not in the living room. Just you follow me, and I will take you to it."

Mr. Stevens stood and then went into the hall, Dawn just a few feet behind him. Instead of turning towards the front of the house Mr. Stevens headed towards the back door. Once outside, he walked around behind the garage to the edge of their lawn.

Dawn temporarily forgot her bad news. Her hand flew to her face, and she let out an audible gasp.

"Is that for me?" she managed, talking and walking at the same time.

"It's for you. Happy graduation. I thought you might need a way to get to the farm and back this summer. If you're working for the Elwood's, that is."

Dawn ran to the small two-door Plymouth roadster sitting on the well-manicured lawn. It was a bright blue color with scarcely a mark on it. Someone had taken care of the old two-door.

"It's a 1936 model, and it belonged to a school teacher in Gainesville. She traded it in, and my friend at Jim Douglas Chevrolet over in High Springs called me. I had told him to be on the lookout for me. With the war on, used cars are getting hard to find. No new ones are being made this year either, you know. I doubt there will be any more cars made until this war is over."

"Oh, Daddy, it's beautiful. I'm going to get my license tomorrow."

"I think we better have a few lessons before then, Baby. I'll drive you out to the football field parking lot, and you can practice there."

Two weeks later watermelon season was in full swing. A young man from town had been hired to take Jim's place in the field. Dawn was excited to be able to drive to the Elwood's farm in her own car. She no longer helped with the water but now had the wonderful job of helping Jim's mother. She began calling her future mother-in-law Mrs. Elwood, but now that she was graduated from High School Mrs. Elwood insisted that Dawn call her Janice.

Janice was teaching her how to tend the garden and how to cook and lots of other wonderful things that had to do with keeping house. Dawn had never had the chance to learn those skills as they had all been done by Elissa. She and Janice had grown very close. Janice replacing Dawn's mother and Dawn becoming the daughter Janice had always wanted but could not have.

Dawn wanted to be Jim's wife, and Jim wanted to be a farmer like his dad. She asked Janice question after question about farm life and being a farmer's wife. They also talked about Jim, his likes and dislikes. Janice told her stories from when Jim was small, and they were like treasures she put in her heart.

June came, and the weather grew hotter. Dawn began to think something had happened to Jim because there had been no letters since he had left Camp Blanding. Janice was nervous too, but she tried to stay calm in front of Dawn.

"Don't worry, Dawn. Jim's alright. Think of it this way. If something had happened to him, the army would have notified James, Sr. and me. We've heard nothing either. I believe he will write as soon as he is allowed to."

"It scares me not to hear from him. This waiting is torture."

"I know. Let's both pray tonight and see if something doesn't happen."

After supper that Tuesday night Dawn and her daddy sat in front of the old Philco and tuned in to the Mutual Radio Network. It had become their habit to listen to Gabriel Heatter report on the war. Many Americans loved this "There's good news tonight," approach. The news was electric that night. The Allied Command had invaded France and were already pushing the Germans back. The amphibious landing involved close to 7,000 vessels from various Allied countries. The landing had taken place in the first few minutes of June 6, 1944. Heavy casualties were reported at the five beaches along the 50 or so miles of Normandy, France.

As Mr. Heatter gave out the facts of the long-anticipated invasion, Dawn's face and spirits fell further and further. Her daddy was intensely listening to the news and failed to notice Dawn's sudden withdrawal. When she could stand it no longer, she left the room without speaking and climbed the stairs to her bedroom where she could write and cry in private.

Dear Diary, This is the second worse day of my life. I've not heard from Jim since he left Camp Blanding and tonight I found out that the U.S. suffered heavy losses in the invasion of France. I'm certain that Jim must have been in that invasion. It would explain why I've not heard anything from him. What if he's one of the casualties? What if he's ... I can't write it. I mustn't think it. Oh, Diary, what am I going to do?

Wednesday, Thursday and Friday came and went. Every day Dawn went to the Elwood farm and worked alongside Janice. Neither one could cheer up the other, so they busied themselves with the farmhouse chores and spoke little of Jim. Janice had not received any mail from Jim or the Army which Janice thought was a good sign.

"I'm sure if Jim were hurt or something, the Army would notify us. That gives me hope."

"You'll let me know if you hear from them, won't you?"

"Of course, Dear. It's in God's hands. Let him take care of it. When Jim left, I asked God to take care of him, and I feel that God's answer was yes."

Saturday afternoon Dawn came home early. The last watermelons were put on trucks and all the equipment put away. Dawn was sad because she would not have a good reason to visit Janice until tobacco season. Much to her surprise, a letter was lying on the small table in the living room. It was addressed to her and had stamps and marks with labels all over the front of it. She looked at the return address. It was from an Army FPO, and it was in Jim's handwriting. Dawn did not wait to run upstairs to read but ripped the envelope opened and read it standing right where she was.

Dearest Dawn, Please forgive me for not writing before now. We have been busy training, and they said no mail could go out until the first week of June. Something is going on, but no one knows what. There's one rumor for nearly every soldier. Because of that, we don't know what is happening. This much we do know, Divisions are leaving every few hours. They pick them up in trucks with all their gear and disappear. I think we may be in combat soon. I'm not sure I will be able to tell you anything about it, but when it's over, I will write you.

I miss you terribly. I still get your letters even though I wasn't able to respond. I'm so happy that you and Mom hit it off so well. I miss her cooking something awful. I guess you are about done with melons now. Will you get a job this summer or wait and work at the farm during the tobacco season.

Now I want to tell you how much I love you...

The only thing that really got through to Dawn was the knowledge that it was possible Jim was not in the D-Day invasion. She opened the desk and pulled out her stationery and immediately began the happiest letter she had written in weeks.

Later she reread Jim's letter again and again. She read it through tears and smiles almost at the same time. She thought about his tobacco question. Her daddy wanted her to get a job, maybe even as a teller at the bank, but she didn't know if she could give up seeing Janice. She wanted to work at the farm during the tobacco season. She could work in the fields or help in the garden and with the meals for the workers. There would be a large number for the tobacco crop.

She lay back on the bed, holding Jim's letter over her heart and thought about the first year she had worked with him during the tobacco season. Her first thought was how hot it was. She remembered how the sweat stuck to her shirt, revealing her undergarment and it was embarrassing. There were two other girls stringing the tobacco leaves and one other one handing the tobacco to the stringers. They looked exactly like she did and paid no attention. By the end of the week, Dawn forgot all about it. White shirts were cooler, and that's what everyone wore, including the men who just had Tee-shirts on.

Her job was to take the long tobacco leaves out of the wooden sled two or three at a time. She put the stems together so that the stems were even and then handed them to one of the girls who was tying the tobacco on the long sticks. At first, she was clumsy, and she was sure she was so slow that Mr. Elwood would tell her to go home.

Jim was working in the field, cropping the largest leaves on the first pass through. The big leaves were worth a lot of money and the sale of this crop would be the family's largest income for the year. Dawn was just happy to be at the farm and near Jim. It was their sophomore year, and they had started going steady at the end of that summer's watermelon season. Jim was all Dawn could think about.

Between hands, she would look up to see if she could see him straightening up in the field. Except for watermelon and tobacco season, they met at the movie theater every Saturday and sat together, holding hands and sharing popcorn.

It was after the tobacco season that year that she knew for sure she was in love. The actual event took place Saturday evening on their way home from the movies. That particular day the movie theater had run a split double show. The first movie was a western as usual but the second was a love story. The very nature of the film left Dawn feeling warm and cozy. She could tell something was different inside her, but she had no idea what it was. Due to the length of the movie, it was nearing dark when they left the theater.

The two couples' walk home took them past the drug store, and for the first time, the boys suggested they stop and get a sundae. As far as the girls were concerned this was added romance to an already romantic charged day. Each couple sat side by side in one of the back booths, and both couples found it hard to eat their sundaes with only one hand. They made sure of course that no one was looking.

It was only a few blocks to where the girls lived, but the couples took their time. The large oaks that lined the sidewalks provided cover from the setting sun and added their own help with limiting vision. When they reached the corner which was the edge of Dawn's lawn, Blair and Charlotte walked on ahead to Charlotte's house. Jim paused under the large live oak on the corner itself, his eyes on the retreating couple. When they were several feet away, he turned to look at Dawn. She looked back. She saw what she felt in his eyes. Jim put his other hand on her shoulder and slowly pulled her towards him. She was powerless to stop the motion, powerless to do anything but lift her lips toward his.

The kiss was over in a moment, but the memory lasted for days. Later that night, Dawn lay in her bed too hyped to sleep. Over and over she replayed the embrace in her mind. She could feel the strength of his body against hers, the strength of his arms pulling her closer and closer. She remembered closing her eyes and tilting her head. When his lips met hers she thought she would have fallen if he had not been holding her so close. Heat ran through her body and reached her heart which subsequently melted.

When he released her and removed his lips, she held on for a few seconds. She was afraid to let go. She wanted him to do it again, but she knew he wouldn't because someone might see them and he wanted to protect her. He did look straight into her eyes, and his lips moved.

"I love you, Dawn. I will always love you."

It was the most wonderful moment of her life at that point and the most wonderful words she had ever heard. Lying in bed, she wished she had told him she loved him too.

Jim

On June 6th while the invasion of Normandy and France was underway, Jim Elwood sat on his folding army cot, a piece of plywood for a desk; his hand with the pen poised over the last sheet of paper. The 83rd Infantry Division had just received word that they were shipping out after evening chow. The Division Commander had made it clear that if they wanted to send any word home, this would be their last opportunity.

Jim wasn't sure what to write to Dawn. He had written a short note to his mom and dad. There was little he could say except that they were shipping out. No one would say where, though rumors were rampant. To a soldier, the 83rd believed their destination was France. The invasion was underway, and once a beachhead was secured more men would be needed to push the Germans out of France.

Jim chewed on the end of the pen and started to write several times. He knew anything he said would likely cause Dawn more worry. He thought it quite likely that he would be killed within the next week or two and he didn't want Dawn to stop living as well. He wanted to tell her to go on with her life. When something happened to him, he wanted her to find another man and be happy. He felt sad and at the same time proud that he was helping the world to be free of a tyrant. He had known when he volunteered that death was a real possibility. He took another deep breath and began to write.

That night the division moved from the hinder land of England to the English coast near Plymouth. The trucks bounced over the neglected roads all through the night and sleep was next to impossible. Everyone's nerves were on edge and cigarettes were being passed around the Six-by. Jim, like everyone else, had taken up the habit. He held the cigarette, watching the red embers of the burning tobacco and wondered if the leaves had come from his farm or near his community.

Morning found them outside of a recently abandoned tent city. Assignments were quickly made, and the 83rd Division took residence in the temporary quarters. They were told not to get comfortable as they would be leaving as soon as transports were available. Every troop carrying vessel in the theater was involved in the D-Day landing and those still afloat would be back in a matter of hours or days.

Three days later the second phase of the invasion was underway with more troops loading in England and moving across the channel. There were units from England, Canada, and other allied countries in addition to the United States. Jim and his comrades continued to wait their turn. They were allowed to see the mail that caught up with them, but they were forbidden to write letters of their own. The army was keeping its secrets.

The day before the 83rd embarked for France one of Dawn's letters caught up with Jim. He read it over and over, folding it each time and putting it in his breast pocket even though the pocket was supposed to be empty. Once on board the ship, he found a place to sit down and read it again.

Dearest Jim, I miss you so much and wish I could hear from you. I know it must be difficult for you to write or you would. Daddy and I listen to the news every night trying to find out what is happening. There seems to be so little news about the war in Europe, just about the war in the Pacific. I hope you aren't going there; the losses have been just awful. I couldn't stand it if something happened to you, Jim. In truth, I would just want to die myself.

On a happier note, I will be headed for the farm tomorrow for the first day of watermelon season. I'm going to help your mother in the garden and feeding the crew. I'm learning how to cook and sew and keep house. You will be very proud of me. I love driving my little car out to the farm and wish you were here so we could go "park like we did the last weekend before you left. Do you remember when you were kissing me, and you put your arm around me and started to pull my zipper down? I wanted to tell you no, and you kissed me again, and I felt your tongue, and I suddenly couldn't say no. I remember the touch of your hands, so soft even though calloused from the farm. My heart was beating so fast I could hardly breathe, and then you touched...

Jim had a hard time with the rest of the letter. Of course, he remembered that night, the taste of her perfume on the tip of his tongue when he touched it to her ears. She had trembled when he did that, and it had filled him with desire. When alone, he seldom thought about anything else. It made what he was about to do that much harder. He prayed and then was ashamed of being a coward. He was a soldier, and if he was to die for his country, he would do so. But he loved Dawn and the things she wrote in her letter only made him more homesick for her.

By evening they were off the coast of France. The smaller boats took them in by platoons and deposited them on the secured beach. By this time the battle had moved inland and spread out. The 83rd would assemble on the beach, move up to a safe area and wait for orders.

For days Jim and his fellow infantrymen were held behind the front lines as the advance moved ever so slowly forward. Finally, on July 2 they were ordered to march toward the front. There was a lot of joking as the units tried to make light of the situation. For days they had watched the dead and the wounded pass by on their way to the rear lines. It was not a comforting scene.

On Monday, July 3rd they were very close to the front lines. Close enough to hear the artillery shells screaming through the air, both outgoing and incoming. Just waiting played on their nerves. Jim had kept a small New Testament in his back pocket, and every time they stopped to eat or rest he took it out and read it. They had reached the environs of a small village called Sainteny.

On the evening of July 4th, each company was briefed by the company commander. The village was defended by the S.S. Grenadiers of a crack division belonging to the 6th

German Regiment. The 6th, they were told, were hardened paratroopers. Heavy resistance was expected. Later, it would be reported that the 83rd had terrible casualties of over a thousand soldiers and were only able to advance a few yards.

One of those casualties was Private Jim Elwood. A heavy artillery shell landed close to his position and threw him and several others in the air. They were left for dead as their company retreated. During the German countersurge, Jim was discovered still breathing by the S.S. Grenadiers. The soldier who found him ripped his dog tags off and put them in his pocket as a souvenir.

Jim's body was taken behind enemy lines and eventually reached Stalag Luft III. Jim was lucky in this regard since the German Air Force were more lenient than the regular army. This particular stalag became famous after the war due to the great escape that happened there in 1943. The stalags were created to house non-coms and privates who were captured by German forces.

Jim regained consciousness in a medical tent erected in the German rear lines. He awoke lying flat of his back on a makeshift cot with a German officer looking down at him. He had no idea where he was or why he was there. As he searched his mind, he could find knowledge of nothing. His mind was blank. The German officer stood with a clipboard and a pen. When he saw Jim was awake, he began asking questions.

"What is your last name, Private Jim?"

Jim. His name was Jim? Jim what? Nothing came. Not even Jim. As hard as he tried to remember Jim had zero meaning to him.

"I don't know. How do you know my name is Jim?"

"Who is Dawn?"

Jim thought for a minute. He squeezed his eyes tight and concentrated. No Dawn. He couldn't think of the name of one single human being.

"I have no idea. Do you have a last name?"

"No, just Dawn. She wrote you a letter, and you had it in the chest pocket of your shirt. She evidently is your lover. And, you say, you don't remember her."

Jim shook his head. As try as he might, nothing would surface. He could make no connections of any kind. The questioning went on with the same results. Nothing the German officer asked or said made any connection. He found out that he was a prisoner of war, but he had no memory of being in a battle. He could remember nothing of his military experience. It was like starting over, he would learn, beginning at zero. The story of the war and the battle for France would be revealed in his long stay in the stalag.

Dawn

Dawn walked from the mailbox to the front porch. She had just returned home from the farm where she had been helping Mrs. Elwood finish up the garden and the canning of vegetables. She was happy watermelon season was over, but she knew she would be lonely waiting for tobacco season to start. With the University of Florida just a few miles away her daddy had been encouraging her to enroll and make some practical use of her time. He still did not visualize his Dawn as being a farmer's wife.

When Dawn reached the swing, she sat down and held the mail in her hand. She quickly laid her daddy's mail to one side and clasped Jim's letter tightly. She kissed it as if Jim could sense it and then tore the flap loose. It was only one page, but Jim had written on both sides. He had also written with smaller letters than usual.

Dearest Darling Dawn, Today is June 6, and we are on the coast of England. I don't know what is happening, but something is. Ship after ship is leaving the harbor, and each one is loaded with men. We just arrived, so I don't know where we are in the embarking status. No one in authority will answer any questions and while there are plenty of stories I know they are just guesses. One thing I do know is that there are a lot of soldiers of all nationalities getting on ships and heading out to sea. I can only assume we will be going too; I just wish we knew where we were going and what was in store for us. This is my last sheet of paper, and there is no more available. We were told that today would be the last day we could send letters home. I wrote Mom and Dad and saved the last sheet for you.

I don't know what will happen to me, but I want to tell you how much I love you in case you don't hear from me again. If I should be killed in action, I want you to forget me and find someone else and marry them and be happy. That would make me happy. I pray a lot and read my New Testament a lot and I dream a lot. I can't say I'm not afraid because I am. I don't want to die, mostly because I love you so much and want to come home to you and get married and buy a farm.

63

You may not hear from me for some time. Please don't sit home and mope. You will get depressed. I am sure there are lots of opportunities to serve without joining the military. I think you would make a great volunteer. Maybe you could go to The University of Florida and become a nurse and help wounded GIs when they return to the states for treatment. If that happened to me, I sure would be happy to look up and see a beautiful nurse like you.

Dawn's eyes were so wet she could not see the page. Tears were dropping on the paper and washing away the words. The words that were so precious to her. She folded the letter back up and put it in the envelope to finish later when she was not so emotional. Dawn sat on the swing and thought. She discounted Jim's statement about being killed and certainly about her loving someone else. That was impossible, and she would not even give it a moment of her time. She did think about Jim's thoughts on helping out. Maybe she could make her daddy happy and please Jim at the same time.

The next morning after she kissed her daddy goodbye she put on her best outfit and drove the little Plymouth coupe to the Alachua County Hospital in Gainesville. She wished that she could attend the University of Florida but there were very few females there, and she did not want to leave her daddy and go to the college for girls in Tallahassee. She went to the administration office and filled out an application to work at the hospital as a nurse's aide.

The lady that handled her application was gray-headed and wrinkled, but her eyes sparkled, and Dawn liked her immediately.

"Why do you want this job?" the lady asked. "From the look of your clothes, you don't need the little bit of money it pays."

"No Ma'am. I just want to help out. My fiancé is in the army, and he thought I should do something to help out. I thought I might be able to help wounded soldiers or something like that."

"Well, we don't have any injured soldiers right now, but there are some headed for the hospital at Camp Blanding in the very near future we're told. But I don't think they have a training program there; they're mostly hiring trained nurses and aides."

"Then I'll work here and get training, and when I'm trained, I'll go help the soldiers."

"That's a good plan. Would you be able to start next Monday, June 26th?"

"Yes. Monday will be fine. I need to tell my daddy and my fiancé's family."

"Be in my office at 7:00 a.m., alright?"

Dawn left the hospital and headed back to Farmville, a song on her lips. For the first time in several weeks, she smiled and thought good thoughts. It was well that she did not know where Jim was at the moment or what was happening to him.

Every day and every night Dawn asked God to protect Jim and bring him home. She wrote a letter every night and mailed it on her way to the hospital every morning. She loved her job and because she was a quick learner was soon given responsibilities of her own. The patients found her careful but tender. She quickly became a hospital favorite with staff and patients, and the nurses took extra time to teach her more than her job required. The days passed, and July 4th came, and Dawn went to the farm to see the Elwood's.

She and Mrs. Elwood had a great time, each trying to cheer up the other. Still, no word about Jim's whereabouts or safety had reached either one of them. Mrs. Elwood was sad to hear that Dawn would not be available when the tobacco season began, but she shared Dawn's excitement about the hospital job. She was a good listener as Dawn related all the things she was learning to do and how much she like helping sick people. They would not see each other for another two weeks.

Then, on July 18th, Dawn pulled her coupe into its parking place beside the house. She had seen Mrs. Elwood's vehicle alongside the curb in front of the house as she arrived. Her heart skipped a beat as she made her way to the back door and then into the living room. Mrs. Elwood was sitting on the large chair Dawn's mother had loved. She held a glass of iced tea in one hand and an envelope in the other. Dawn was sure she saw the faintest trace of tears at the edge of Mrs. Elwood's eyes.

Dawn stopped walking, her eyes moving from Mrs. Elwood's face to the yellow envelope she was grasping in her left hand.

"Is it Jim?"

"Yes. It's about Jim."

"Tell me, please."

"I can't. I'll let you read it."

Dawn walked over and took the envelope. Standing next to the large chair she opened the flap of the Western Union envelope and pulled the small sheet out. Her eyes ran through the message hurriedly, not pausing at the STOPs. Slowly, the message fluttering from her hand, she sank to the floor, collapsing in a heap.

"Elissa," Mrs. Elwood called out, "bring a wet cloth. Hurry."

Mrs. Elwood knelt beside Dawn, cradling her head in her lap. She could not stop the tears from falling onto Dawn's hair.

Jim

Jim struggled to find some memory to go with his name and the letter from the girl named Dawn. He also struggled from the pain of the various shrapnel wounds on his arms, legs, and back. It was difficult to move, but he could see the white of the bandages. There was an IV in his left arm which was strapped down to the cot. He knew the pain but not its source. What had happened that caused the bandages and throbbing in so many parts of his body? Why couldn't he remember? Anything?

A German medical aide came over to his cot and checked the IV. He then removed the sheet that covered him and examined the bandages. Satisfied he put the sheet back and left. Jim wanted to talk, but he already knew that the aide spoke only German. The two men on either side of him were also German and spoke no English. Jim wanted to ask how much longer he would be in the makeshift hospital, but the doctor who spoke English had not returned for several days. Jim also wanted the doctor to read the letter to him again. Perhaps he would remember something.

One day followed the one before, and bit by bit the bandages were removed, first one and then another. The IV was gone, and someone was feeding him soft foods. Then finally, an aide helped him get up, and he took his first steps in weeks. It was a struggle. His muscles were weak, and the pain was sharp, but he gritted his teeth and moved his legs forward.

Around the first of October, the hospital discharged him, and he was put on a transport with two English prisoners and taken to the barracks inside the stalag itself. Jim was assigned a hut with ten other American POWs. Introductions started.

"Hello, welcome to the Ritz. I'm Sgt. Marty Sheldon."

"Hello, thank you. I'm Jim."

"Jim what?"

"I don't know. I can't remember anything. I have a letter to Jim. It's from a girl named Dawn. I don't have the envelope, so I don't know last names or addresses. I don't know who I am and I don't know who she is. I'm afraid I don't know anything."

"What about your dog tags?" Sgt. Sheldon asked.

"I don't have any dog tags

One by one the other nine prisoners introduced themselves. Jim tried to attach faces and names. He was anxious to rebuild some memory, and he latched on to every piece of information available. One of the things that hit him right away was how thin the other POWs were. He was below his usual weight, but the food at the hospital had been nutritious. The second thing that struck him was the condition of the uniforms the men were wearing. Not just the stains and dirt but the tears and worn spots. It was obvious that life was going to be hard in the stalag.

Actually, it was not as hard as some stalags but was worse than it would have been if not for the previous escape attempts there.

Dawn

Thanksgiving came, and Dawn convinced her daddy to accept the Elwood's invitation to celebrate the holiday at the farm. Every night since the telegram had come Dawn had called Mrs. Elwood to see if she had learned anything else. The telegram had said Jim was Missing-In-Action rather than killed, but in a way, the not knowing was almost worse than knowing. The army assumed he had been taken prisoner or if he was dead his body could have been taken by the Germans for other reasons. There were plenty of tales that was for sure.

The Elwood's wanted to know about Dawn's work at the hospital, and Dawn enjoyed telling about what was happening.

"They've been sending me all over the hospital. I worked in the main ward for a while and then in recovery, and now I'm in the nursery. I get to see about the new mothers and rock the new babies. It is so much fun. As soon as Jim is back, I'm..."

She couldn't hold the tears back. Some days were like that. Happy and then sad. Her daddy jumped up and put his arms around her. Mrs. Elwood reached across the table and patted her hand. Mr. Elwood excused himself and went into a back room. Thanksgiving suddenly took on a different tone.

"Dawn, I know it's hard. Believe me, I live this every day and so does Jim's dad. But today we can be thankful that Jim may still be alive. Other mothers and girlfriends have not been so lucky."

Dawn got control of her emotions, wiped her eyes with the soft cloth napkin in her lap and tried to smile. In a few minutes, everything was back to normal.

"I heard this week that Camp Blanding is now receiving wounded soldiers at their hospital. It may become the largest hospital in the state of Florida before they're done. I want to apply to work there. What do you think?" Dawn asked.

"You'd have to move near there, it's too far to drive isn't it?" asked Mrs. Elwood.

"You'd leave me?" Dawn's daddy asked.

"I'd come home on weekends, Daddy. Elissa will take care of you, and I'm a big girl now. It's time I tried my wings don't you think?"

"Well, as long as you're home on weekends. I don't want to spend every Saturday and Sunday worrying about what you're doing."

Mr. Elwood joined the conversation, "What makes you want to do this, Dawn? I thought you really liked the County Hospital. We like seeing you on a regular basis; you've become like a part of our family."

Dawn looked around the table and took in the love and concern on the faces. She felt the same way about all of them, but she was drawn to the soldiers and their possible needs.

"I think it's that I feel like I can best honor Jim's sacrifice by helping his fellow soldiers who also have made a sacrifice. It's something I can do and because I can, I must."

Mrs. Elwood looked up from her pumpkin pie and smiled across at Dawn. "When are you thinking on doing this, Sweetheart?"

"I want to do it so I can start at the beginning of next year, so I'm applying the first of next month."

In January 1945, Dawn went to work at the Camp Blanding Hospital. The hospital was already crowded with wounded G.I.s. Dawn was assigned as an aide on one of the ambulatory wards and soon found herself busier than she could have imagined. Many of the patients were recovering from serious wounds and needed someone to help them walk. Dawn threw herself into her work in an effort not only to help the returning soldiers but to keep the dread thoughts out of her head.

Dawn volunteered to work extra hours and soon was involved in a program that made visits to the hospital at night, reading to those who couldn't read, playing cards, checkers and other games to help pass the time for those recovering. It helped her as well.

On weekends she would go home and see her daddy and the Elwood's. The constant talk was about Jim and the lack of word on what had happened to him. Slowly the Allies were moving the Germans back, and prisoners of war were being recovered, but so far Jim had not been found. These MIA discussions were hard on Dawn, as she felt Jim's parents might be slowly giving up. She didn't want them to give up as she never entertained the idea of giving up, herself. She was sure she would know if Jim was dead.

She told her daddy, James, and Janice that she knew Jim was alive.

She said, "There is no way Jim could be dead and I not know it. He's alive, and I don't want anyone to talk about him not being alive."

She said that and she believed it, but still there was that small nagging doubt; an evil voice in her head that said if he was alive they would know it by now. Another voice, somewhat encouraging, said that the opposite was true; if he was dead, they would have found his body by now.

Jim

The temperature at Stalag Luft 3 was freezing, and six inches of snow was on the ground when the Soviet troops drove to within 16 miles of the stalag. Jim along with 11,000 other POWs were marched out of the camp a little before midnight, the night of January 27, 1945. It was a tough march of over 30 miles to a town where they were allowed to rest for almost three days. Then they walked another 15 miles to a train station. They were then shipped to Stalag VII-A at Moosburg. They remained at Stalag VII-A until early April.

Jim was lucky in that he had had excellent care in the German hospital and by the time the marches began he had fully recovered physically. Lack of proper food and the harshness of the weather took its toll on all the prisoners, and many were lost along the way. Later it was discovered that many of the lost had just wandered off and the Germans let them go. The fight had gone out of the German army.

Stalag VII-A had been designed to hold around 15,000 prisoners of war but due to the other stalags being evacuated its numbers swelled to well over a hundred thousand. The barracks were overwhelmed, and some prisoners wound up in tents and others in ditches. There was comfort in numbers, and the various POWs took heart in the knowledge that the Allied forces were closing in on the Germans.

Their dream of liberation came true in April of that year. The 14th Armored Division of the United States Army overcame the stalag on the 29th of April. The slow process of rehabilitation began with the badly sick and wounded moved to field hospitals first. Jim began to gain his strength back with the food now being served from the Division's field kitchens. First, the doctors and then the officers examined Jim and were left wondering what to do with him. Jim was still not able to recall his past.

It was determined that he was from the south due to his accent but just where was not known. Ultimately, it was decided that he would be sent to a hospital with a psychiatric wing for evaluation and hopefully a clue to his identity. On May 8 the entire armed forces celebrated the end of the war in Europe. Even though Jim could not remember his part in the fighting, he was just as glad as the rest of the forces. He lived in the hope that he would soon discover who he was and what he was supposed to do with his life. Jim finally made it to a ship bound for Charleston, South Carolina in early June.

From the ship, they were moved to a train and within an hour were on their way south. Jim sat next to a window and watched the scenery in hopes he would see something that would trigger his memory. After an hour of slowly making their way out of Charleston and the surrounding area, his eye was caught by something growing in a field next to the tracks. It was gone before he could get a good look, but he sensed that he knew what it was. He pushed his face against the glass and stared intently hoping for another opportunity to view whatever it was.

Then, there it was again. Not very far along yet but the shape of the plants were unmistakable. Jim squeezed his eyes in consecration. He knew it. He knew that plant. The word burst right out of his mouth, "Tobacco," he said, and he said it again. Before the next hour had passed, they passed several watermelon fields and again bit by bit the word "watermelon" came to him. He knew those words, and he knew more about those words. He knew things about them. Things like how they were grown and harvested and sold. He was excited. For the first time after his capture, he knew something about himself.

Jim pulled the tattered letter out of his shirt pocket and read it again. Not that he needed to read it to understand it. Every word had been committed to memory. He was reading it again to see if anything would pop out at him. There it was at the beginning of the letter. He read it slowly, letting the words sink in.

"On a happier note, I will be headed for the farm tomorrow for the first day of watermelon season. I'm going to help your mother in the garden and of course, feeding the crew."

He connected the dots. He was from a farm. He had worked in watermelons and tobacco also. He tried hard to visualize his mother and the farm. Then he tried to visualize the girl named Dawn who was helping his mother and whom he had been intimate with. Nothing new was there. But he knew that he came from a place that grew watermelons and tobacco. He turned back to the window and stared again. Maybe another clue would pass by.

The soldiers ate in the train's dining car and slept in the day chairs as the night closed around them. Here and there card games were going on, but for the most part, the troops were tired, and in spite of their being cramped and uncomfortable, they managed to sleep off and on. Sometime in the early morning hours, the train pulled into the station in Jacksonville, Florida. Several ambulatory soldiers got off and headed for other means of transportation to make their way home. Jim was ambulatory, but since he didn't know where home was, he had to stay on board. Somewhere up ahead was a hospital and there he hoped to find help for his faulty memory.

Dawn

A year almost to the day had passed since Dawn had written that letter, and she was once again at the Elwood's farm. Watermelon picking was underway, and she was helping Janice prepare lunch for the workers. It was a Saturday, and she was off from the hospital. The trip to the farm was good for her because the sudden influx of wounded soldiers at the Camp Blanding Hospital had filled her with memories and longings. When she tended one of the seriously wounded soldier, she would suddenly see Jim's face on the battered body.

The Elwood's had settled into a routine of their own, believing their son was alive but at the same time puzzled that the army had not been able to find him. It had become a part of that routine for them not to talk to Dawn about it. They accepted her as part of the family, and she spent as much time with them as their schedules would allow. Janice had not been able to conceive after giving birth to Jim, and her longing for a daughter was now partially fulfilled by the presence of Dawn.

The two women worked side by side, and Dawn kept Janice appraised of what her work was like and how sad it made her to see so many young men in pain, learning to live without arms or legs or an eye. She told about how some wanted to talk about what happened to them, and others would shake their heads when questioned. Dawn had learned to be tender with them, not only in their physical but in their emotional treatment as well.

Monday morning, when she went back to work the head nurse on her wing, sent for her. Puzzled, Dawn made her way to the office at the end of the hall. She knocked on the door and entered when she heard the pleasant voice on the other side. She was greeted with a smile and a request.

"Sit down, Miss Stevens. This is Dr. Filson, Head of Psychiatry. He would like to have a few words with you."

"Good morning Miss Stevens. I'm sure you are wondering what is going on and so I will get straight to the point. I am

76

looking for an aide to work on my wing of the hospital, and your name surfaced as the ideal person for the job."

"I don't know, Dr. Filson. I really like my job, and I feel like I'm helping the soldiers on my wing."

"Yes, I'm sure you are, Miss Stevens, but these men need help as well, and not everyone has the ability to work with them. It is believed that you do. I would like to offer you a three-month trial, and if when the time is over, you want to return to the physically wounded part of the hospital I won't stand in your way."

Dawn hated to tell the doctor no since he had shown such confidence in her, but she wanted to be in the same part of the hospital where the wounded soldiers were, just in case Jim was to be sent there. If he did come to Camp Blanding Hospital she could always transfer back, she reasoned.

"I'll give it a try, Dr. Filson, but I don't know anything about working with mental patients."

"These aren't 'mental' patients, Miss Stevens, just emotionally wounded ones. They need tenderness and compassion. You do know about those methods from all I've learned about you."

Arrangements were made for Dawn to transfer to the Psychiatric Ward. She was apprehensive but determined to make the best of it; to at least give it her best attempt. First, she went and told all her former patients good-bye. They were, of course, disappointed that she was leaving them. Not only was she an excellent aide, she was very beautiful.

By the end of the week, Dawn had settled in. She found the new job very challenging and a lot different. Some of the patients also had physical wounds which she cared for, but as she came to know each patient, she began to feel an attachment to them and the difficulties each was facing.

When Friday came, she was stopped by Dr. Filson as she entered the special wing. "Miss Stevens, may I have a word with you?"

"Yes, Sir."

"During the night we received two new patients. I'm assigning one of them to you. Its a special case but I think you might be of great help in this particular situation."

"I'll try my best, Doctor. What is different about this patient?"

"I have his chart. Read it carefully, and then I'll introduce you to the young man." With that Dr. Filson handed over the medical chart he was holding in his left hand. He stood quietly while she read the contents of the folder. He was surprised when her eyes opened wide, and a gasp escaped her pursed lips. He thought she might faint and he reached out to steady her.

"What is it, Miss Stevens? What's wrong?"

"This Jim, he doesn't know who he is?"

"No, he didn't even know his name was Jim, but a letter he had was addressed to a Jim, so that's the name he's been using."

"Oh, God! Could it be...I have to see him, Dr. Filson. Take me to him please."

"Certainly, Miss Stevens, he's at the end of the wing on the left-hand side. I expect he's sitting in a chair looking out a window. Come with me, and I'll introduce you."

Dawn found it hard to breathe as they went out of the office and across to the special wing. She knew it was ridiculous to believe it might be her Jim and yet, the idea of a letter addressed to a "Jim"...she knew she had sent such a letter. She never thought to ask whose name signed the letter. Perhaps Dr. Filson had not even seen the letter. They entered the ward and the unusual sight of patients sitting and standing caught her off guard.

She moved around the patients trying to get a view of the soldier at the far end of the hall who was sitting in a chair, his back to the busy activity occurring on the wing. Dawn froze. It was Jim's profile. She was sure of it. She took more hesitant steps, her eyes fixated on the thin patient facing the window. If he would only look her way, she would be sure. Her steps hastened, and before she thought about it, she was running down the long wing to the last bed on the left.

"Jim," she called. "Jim, it's me, it's Dawn."

The patient known only as Jim turned slowly in his chair. No recognition showed on his face, no emotion lit up his eyes. He seemed stunned as he was. Who was this nurse's aide running toward him and shouting his name? Then her name broke through his muddled thoughts. He knew the name, Dawn. It was one of the few names he did know. He knew the name, but he had no recognition of the person named Dawn. He knew her words. He had cherished her words, but he had no idea of who she was nor of the meaning of what she had written. He had no memory of any of it.

The aide was beautiful. He also knew that much. He did not know what to do when she arrived at his chair and threw her arms around him. She held him so tight he almost couldn't breathe, and he couldn't move his arms. He felt her body shake, and then he heard the sobs. Slowly, she raised her head and then her arms and then her body and looked at him, pain in her face. He looked back, his face a question mark.

"You don't know me, do you, Jim?" she asked.

"No, Ma'am. I don't. It seems like you know me and I guess I should know you."

"Your name is Jim Elwood, and you are from Farmville, Florida."

"Elwood? My name is Elwood?

"Yes. You father is James Elwood, and your mother is Janice."

"Excuse me, I'm sorry. it's too much information. I have to think. Are you the Dawn in my letter?"

"Yes, my love, I am. I've missed you terribly. We've had no information about you at all. I have to go call your mom and dad. I'll be right back."

Dawn kissed him on the cheek and then turned and fled back up the hall. Dr. Filson tried to flag her down but gave up and moved quickly after her. This was a totally unexpected reaction and incident. A sudden change of mind turned him around and sent him back to the chair where

Jim Elwood was sitting in obvious confusion. His face was a little red as he recalled the words of Dawn's letter.

"Do you have any recollection of Dawn or the information she gave you?" Dr. Filson asked.

"No, Doctor. But something is there; I can sense there is something there, back in my mind somewhere, but it won't come out. She's beautiful isn't she?"

"Yes, she is, and I think she loves you very much. Give it some time. As more information comes to bear, your subconscious will deal with it. Somewhere in your brain, the memory is there; we just have to coax it out."

"Well, I hope it's sooner rather than later; I'm tired of not knowing who I am and what I've done. It's worse now because someone knows who I am and I don't."

Ten minutes after she left Dawn was back. "I've told your parents, Jim, and they will be here as soon as they can."

"What can you tell me about my parents; right now I don't have any memory at all of them.

"Hmm, you look a lot like your dad, and your mother is petite. She has short, brown hair because she works outside in the heat a lot. She has beautiful dark eyes and the world's friendliest smile. Both of them are hard workers as you would expect from farmers."

"Do they grow watermelons and tobacco?"

"Yes, they do. Do you remember?"

"You mentioned watermelons in your letter, and I saw tobacco growing from the train on my way here. I recognized it, but I didn't know why."

Dr. Filson excused himself, and Dawn moved to sit on the edge of Jim's bed. Soon they were lost in conversation about watermelon growing and tobacco farming. Jim asked questions and occasionally nodded his head as if he understood the explanation. Dawn was so happy just to be near her lost love that she forgot for a while that he didn't really know who she was.

Time flew by, the two of them lost in the process of getting acquainted and reacquainted. Their conversation was interrupted by a cry from several feet up the aisle.

"Jim! Oh, Jim, you're back."

Dawn jumped up from the bed and attempted to get between Janice and Jim. She could see what was about to happen. Jim stood up from his chair with a look of surprise and fear on his face. He knew they were coming, but he wasn't mentally prepared to meet parents he didn't recognize. Not true, he thought. He did have a feeling that he knew the faces just like he had felt he knew Dawn. He just couldn't connect the feeling of recognition with any specific memory. It was like seeing someone you vaguely knew but hadn't seen in years. It was the feeling that he should know them, but he couldn't make it out.

In spite of Dawn's effort, Janice reached Jim and threw her arms around him. Jim couldn't decide whether to hug her back and so he moved his hands up and back, almost staggering under the weight of his mother's embrace. Janice held on and wept. James gently took his wife's shoulders and slowly pulled her away. Tears were in his own eyes as well, but he controlled his impulse to grab his son in a bear hug. Dawn had made it clear that Jim would probably not recognize them. His heart wanted to pour out his feelings of relief and thanksgiving, but somehow his mind took charge, and he put out his hand which Jim took.

"We're glad your safe and back home, Jim. Things are going to be alright now. I'm sure this is as much a shock to you as it is to us. Would you be willing to tell us what happened after you lost your memory? We've had no information at all. Were you wounded badly?"

Dr. Filson showed up with extra chairs, and everyone took a seat. Janice insisted that Jim sit next to her on the bed and James and Dawn took chairs across from the two of them. Jim began his story from the time he woke up in the Stalag hospital. He had reached the part where they were put on a train to Stalag VII-A when Dr. Filson joined their small group to tell them that the visiting hours were over and the ward had to shut down for the night. No one wanted to break up the gathering, especially Janice.

She hugged Jim one more time, and the three visitors reluctantly left the ward. James Elmore reminded his wife that they had livestock and other matters that had to be attended to and it would be late when they got home. She nodded, but she couldn't keep the tears from streaming down her face. She hugged Dawn tightly and tried to bring up a smile. "I'll be over sometime tomorrow. I'm going to bring some pictures to share with Jim. Maybe they will stir up his memory. I'm just glad he's safe."

"I'm going to bring some things tomorrow as well," Dawn said.

Mr. Elmore managed to give Dawn an awkward hug before he opened the truck door for Janice. "Thanks again for calling so quickly, Dawn. Things are going to be alright, I'm sure."

The rest of the week saw visits from both the Elmore's in addition to Dawn's daily work in Jim's ward. Janice brought pictures from Jim's younger years as well as views of the farm and the animals. Dawn brought her letters from Jim and each day read one or two of them in hopes that Jim would have a positive reaction to something he had said about his training and subsequent stay in England. The total impact of the information added to what he was experiencing in his conversations with the three of them. He, himself, felt something was happening to his memory, but it was so disorganized that it still left him in the mental dark.

Saturday afternoon Dawn drove back to Farmville. She wanted to talk to her daddy, and there was something she wanted to get from her old bedroom. She felt she was making progress with Jim and she sensed that his mind just needed a final prod to release the memories that were gathering there. Sunday morning she went to church with Daddy and asked all her friends to be praying for Jim. She wore the dark blue dress, black pumps and carried the small purse just like the day Jim left for the army. After church services, she went to her daddy's favorite restaurant on the square downtown for lunch with him.

They had not seen each other for a week, and she needed to tell him about Jim. "Dawn," he said, "don't worry. True love will win out, and you have true love for him, and I know he had the same for you."

"I want to believe it, Daddy, I do, because I know he is falling in love with me again. I'm glad of that, but I want him to remember everything in our past as well."

"I think he will; just be patient. By the way, I haven't seen that dress in a very long time. You look beautiful in it. Where's it been hiding?"

"Thank you, Daddy. It's the dress I wore when Jim left to go to Camp Blanding. I've been saving it until he came home. I'm wearing it today, and I hope it jars his memory."

"Well, it should jar something. You look like your mother when we got married."

Dawn rose out of her chair and put her arm around her daddy. She kissed the tear running down his cheek. "I miss her too, Daddy. I'm so glad I've got you. I love you very much."

Once they were back at the house, Dawn went upstairs to get her suitcase. She paused by her dresser and then opened the small drawer on the left-hand side. It was where she kept her special things. She moved some aside and then chose her very favorite. Looking in the mirror, she pinned it to her dress, right above her heart.

It seemed like she would never get to the Camp Blanding Hospital. There were too many Sunday Drivers out, and none of them were in a hurry. She parked her coupe as close to the special wing as possible. She started to open the door but stopped to check her lipstick in the rearview mirror. She added just a little to the pink color, the same lipstick she had worn that fateful morning. Satisfied, she said a quick prayer and exited the car.

Dawn started her walk down the aisle past the soldiers on either side. She blushed as she heard a few low whistles. Jim was sitting near the window with his parents, but he heard the whistles. He stood up, his eyes locked on Dawn and then he started towards her. They met halfway down the aisle. Dawn stopped, a smile filled her face. Jim stood, unable to move it seemed, his eyes taking in every inch of the girl in front of him. His eyes filled with tears and trembling he reached out his right hand and with his finger touched the faded rose pinned to Dawn's dress.

"I know you, Dawn Stevens. I know you, and I know who I am."

Dawn burst into tears as well and oblivious to those around them; they came together, their lips locked as tight as their hearts.

The End

"Weeping May Tarry for the Night..."

by Philip Dampier

(Paragraphs one and twenty-five were provided by the Owl Canyon Press's Hackathon)

Beyond the cracked sidewalk, and the telephone pole with layers of flyers in a rainbow of colors, and the patch of dry brown grass there stood a ten-foot high concrete block wall, caked with dozens of coats of paint. There was a small shrine at the foot of it, with burnt out candles and dead flowers and a few soggy teddy bears. One word of graffiti filled the wall, red letters on a gold background: Rejoice!

Hannah stepped back and admired her work. Some of her letters were crooked, and none of them were really perfect, but anyone who could read English could make the word out. They wouldn't understand it, but they would be able to read it. It was such an oxymoron considering the nature of the shrine under the word.

The shrine had been there for almost a week now; time enough for the flowers to die and the candles to burn out. Time enough for one short rain shower, as if there wasn't gloom enough. Hannah came to the wall every day to visit and to shed a new tear. Today was different, however. Today she wrote the word and even added an exclamation mark.

Her brother Billy was dead. No way to change that. She found the truth to be bittersweet, and the sweet part led her to paint the word. She stole the two cans of paint and a brush out of her foster parents' garage. She knew she would be in serious trouble when they found out but the way she figured it that was not new news.

Hannah was two when she came to live with Myrtle and Archer Johnson. Billy had been a baby. She remembered little of the first two or three years, but she remembered almost everything that had happened to her and Billy in the seven years afterward. None of what she remembered was pleasant; most of it was painful.

No one believed her story. The Johnsons were such nice people. Regular churchgoers, volunteers for all sorts of community projects and they gave those two poor little orphans a nice home. Right! Hannah thought. They also beat the stew out of those poor little orphans when no one was looking. Not to mention the sexual abuse. Poor little orphan Billy couldn't take it anymore, and now he didn't have to.

Hannah thought many times about suicide herself but she was either too cowardly, or she was too bull-headed. In spite of what she learned in Sunday School, she knew she hated the Johnsons. She no longer referred to them as momma and daddy but as Mr. and Mrs. It was her way of fighting back. They punished her of course, but of course, she would not give in.

Hannah also thought about running away, but she didn't know where to run. It was one of her three alternatives. The second one was to kill the Johnsons, but she didn't know just how to do it, and something told her it was more wrong than what they did to Billy and her. The third one was to try to exist until she could run away. As of this day, it was the one she chose.

The young pre-teen set the cans up against the block wall and laid her brush on top of the red one. Too dangerous to take everything home. This way the paint's absence might not be noticed. At least not till the Johnson's drove by the freshly painted wall. She hoped that they might not do that for a week or two. She was still grieving about her brother. The way she felt at that moment, she wouldn't stop grieving anytime soon. Not only for Billy but for herself. Her painted word was what she felt for Billy if the Sunday School teacher was right, that is. She had to believe he was.

Billy deserved a place without tears. He had shed enough, that was for sure. The thought of Billy smiling in heaven was a reason to rejoice.

Hannah walked over to where the teddy bears were lying and picked one up. That particular one was Billy's most cherished possession. He got it for Christmas when he was three years old. It came in the mail a week before the Holiday, but the Johnsons never said who sent it. That same year she received a Barbie the same way. She thought she would take the bear to her room and hide it somewhere. It would be like having a part of Billy with her in a way.

She thought again about the bear and doll and how their donor was kept anonymous. She let her mind toss the obvious question around. She knew nothing about her parents. The Johnsons either didn't know or purposely lied about it. Could the presents have come from her mom or dad? And why just that one Christmas? The thoughts added to the sadness and so she pushed them away for later consideration.

It was Friday afternoon, and she had been at the shrine much longer than usual. She put the bear under her arm and hurried down the street to the road that her house was on. She needed to sneak the bear in and get her chores done before the Johnsons got home. The chores included getting things ready for dinner and if that wasn't done there would be hell to pay. Why had she stayed at the wall so long?

That night while the family was eating, Hannah decided to ask the Johnsons about her birth mother and real father. Her opening came when Mrs. Johnson asked if she had been by the wall.

"Did you go to the shrine again today, Hannah?"

"Yes, Ma'am."

"I think it's time for you to move on. You can't undo what's been done."

"I miss him so much. He was my only true relative."

"We're your parents, Hannah. We took the two of you in when you lost your parents."

"When I was at the wall I thought about our parents. Will you please tell me about them?"

"Your mother and father didn't want you and put you in a home. We took you in as foster children. You're very lucky."

Hannah had trouble concentrating on washing and drying the dishes when the meal was over because she couldn't stop thinking about what Mrs. Johnson had said to her. The Johnsons only wanted her so they could abuse her and her mother and father didn't want her at all. She couldn't help the tears that ran down her cheeks any more than she could help the hurt in her heart.

Hannah wondered if she looked like her mother. She knew she didn't look like Billy and so one of them must look like their mother and one their father. She hoped she looked like her mother. She walked by the mirror hanging on the kitchen door and studied her face. What would she look like if she were twenty years older? Did her mother have light brown hair like her's? Did she have freckles on her face?

That night, holding Billy's bear, Hannah looked up at the ceiling. Somewhere up there, far away, was her brother. Maybe he was with God. She wished she was with God too. No pain and crying. No shame like she felt now, and if the Sunday School teacher was right, there was real love in heaven. She wondered what that would be like. She closed her eyes and tried to imagine it.

Her lips began to move, and words came out of her mouth.

"God, if you are really up there, will you please love my brother? I love him, and he loves me, but now we're not together anymore."

She was shocked. She had tried to pray but was never able to. She felt emboldened by her beginning and continued.

"Also God, could you send someone to love me? I'm very lonely now that Billy is gone."

Hannah thought about what Mrs. Johnson had said about the wall and moving on. She couldn't move on; that was the problem. Billy was all she had, and now the wall was all there was to remember Billy by besides the bear. She wasn't ready to give the wall up yet. She knew she wouldn't be able to go again until Sunday afternoon. It would have to do.

****

Across town in a small one-room apartment, Mary Elizabeth put the newspaper down. The tears were making it impossible to read, and her heart had taken in all it could stand for a moment. The newspaper had a picture of Billy Johnson and also one of the shrine at the wall. She knew it was her Billy even though she had not seen him since he and Hannah had been taken from her arms ten years before. Billy looked just like the man who had fathered him.

Five of those ten years she had spent in the state women's prison in the northern part of the state. The last five she had spent trying to finish her parole and saving every dime she could. Three weeks ago she had moved back to the city where she had given birth to her two children. Mary Elizabeth had given up hope of getting her children back, and now one of them was dead.

Suddenly, a thought came to her. She went into the bathroom and washed her face and dried her eyes. Sunday was her day off, and she could try to find the wall with the candles and bears. She decided to go to bed early instead of reading. She couldn't afford a television as of yet, but she had her eye on another job that would pay more if they would hire ex-cons.

Lying in bed, Mary Elizabeth tried to focus her thoughts. She wanted to see Hannah as she had seen Billy. She had frozen her daughter's face in her memory, but that was a picture taken ten years ago. She tried to imagine what she would look like now. She would be twelve now and turning into a young woman. It was frustrating not to be able to visualize her as she was now.

Hannah would have been in her foster home for ten years now. She would have a mother and father and love them and be loved. Mary Elizabeth realized Hannah would not only not know her, but she also would not care about her. Best to leave things alone. Maybe later, when Hannah was in high school or college, she might be interested in meeting her birth mother.

The next afternoon an automobile pulled up and parked beside the concrete wall. The driver opened the door but did not get out of the car. Although her face was in shadow, it was easy to tell she was sad. There was something about how she turned away from the sun and rested the weight of her hands on the steering wheel, something about her silent composure that caused Hannah to sigh. The young girl watched the driver lean out of the car and stretch her hand out towards one of the burned out candles.

It was then that Hannah saw the woman's face. The woman's outstretched hand pushed her light brown hair from her eyes exposing a lightly freckled face and light green eyes. Hannah gasped. The woman looked like her; just like she had imagined when she stared at her face in the kitchen mirror.

Mary Elizabeth moved in her seat, swinging her legs out of the interior of the sedan. She leaned forward and stepped out of the car. She was not very steady on her feet, and Hannah saw a tear slowly moving down the woman's cheek and fall on the ground. The young girl's heart stopped for a second, and she moved from the shadow of the large oak to the left of the shrine.

Mary Elizabeth caught the motion in the edge of her vision and turned her head. She had not realized anyone was at the shrine but her. Something caught in her throat. She had trouble breathing and swallowing. The candles, flowers, and bears were temporarily forgotten. She knew this girl. This girl was exactly like the image in her picture box of her when she was in the sixth grade.

Neither of the two spoke; they just stared at the other. For both of them, it was like looking in a time-travel machine's window. One looking ahead and one looking behind. Both wanted to speak but were afraid. Slowly, the two strangers began to walk towards each other, both excited and afraid. What if what they were thinking wasn't true?

Mary Elizabeth spoke first. "Hannah, is that you? Are you Hannah Willis?"

Hannah shook her head, confused. "I'm Hannah, but my last name isn't Willis. At least I don't think it is. I go by Johnson, but that's not my real name. I don't know my real name."

"Are you a foster child?"

"Yes, Ma'am, I am. I live with the Johnsons."

Mary Elizabeth's heart skipped for the third or fourth time.

"Was Billy your brother?"

"Yes, Ma'am, he was. Who are you?

"My name is Mary Elizabeth Willis. I think I might be your mother."

"Mary Elizabeth? You do look like me, but I think my mother must be dead or something."

"Why do you think that, Hannah?"

"Because after she gave Billy and me up we never heard from her, and the Johnsons never talk about her as if she was alive."

"I had two children; a girl named Hannah, and a baby named Billy. I had to let them...no; I had to let you go because I was sent to prison and couldn't take care of you. I had no one to leave you with."

"You went to prison? What for?"

"I was involved with your father, and we were caught trying to get some scrap metal so we could buy milk for Billy and baby food for you."

"They put you in jail for trying to feed us?"

"Yes. Both of us had been in trouble before. Before you were born, and they gave your father twenty years and me ten. I was paroled after five years, and now I'm living here in town."

Mary Elizabeth closed the gap between the two of them. She leaned down just a bit to be on a level with Hannah.

"I thought about the two of you every day since the social worker took you away ten years ago. I never thought I would see either of you again. I won't see Billy, of course, but here you are. Oh my God, he does answer prayer."

"You prayed to see me?"

"Oh yes, night after night. I prayed that the two of you would be safe and have a good home, someone to love you like I do."

Hannah stepped back, confusion from within showing on her face. "He didn't hear you if that's what you prayed. No one loved Billy but me, and no one loved me, but Billy, and now he's gone."

"What about your foster parents, Hannah, surely they love you."

"No. They only wanted us for what they could get. They beat us both unless we did what they said. They made us do terrible things. It's awful. I wish I was dead like Billy."

The tears came then. Tears long held back. Bitter tears of anguish and suffering and embarrassment and mostly anger.

Mary Elizabeth reached out instinctively and pulled Hannah into her arms. Overcome with emotion she too began to cry. They stood that way until the tears began to subside, then Hannah pulled back.

"Are you really my mother?" Hannah asked.

"I'm sure of it Hannah. Everything fits, and you look just like me at your age."

"Can I come live with you?" Hannah asked.

Mary Elizabeth separated herself from Hannah and took a long look at her. She wasn't at all prepared for the question, and the bluntness of it shocked her. Mary Elizabeth had to think about that. She had not come prepared to make such a decision. Would the court give her custody after all that had happened? If so, could she take care of Hannah on the salary she was making? Would a social worker approve of the small apartment she was living in? No way to find out on Sunday. Then some of what Hannah had said began to seep through to her consciousness.

"You said they made you do terrible things. What do you mean, terrible things?"

"You know, sexual things. Billy couldn't stand it. That's why he killed himself."

"No, Hannah! I thought it was an accidental overdose."

"No, Ma'am. He couldn't handle the beatings or the..." Hannah was unable to finish the sentence. Tears were followed by sobs, and before either of them knew it, Mary Elizabeth enveloped Hannah in her arms again.

Her mind was racing. If these accusations were true or even partially true, then something had to be done and done right away. But what? She was an ex-con on parole; who would listen to her? It was Sunday, none of the state offices were opened. If she took Hannah with her, they might accuse her of kidnapping and with her record that could mean a long time in prison.

She let go of Hannah so that she could open her purse. She removed the cheap cell phone from its pocket and looked at her contacts. Angus Cauthen was listed near the top. She pushed the call portion of the screen. Angus was her parole officer and was supposed to be available if she needed him. She certainly needed him.

Ten minutes later Hannah was telling Angus her story. With each sentence, his face grew darker, and his eyes narrowed to slits. When Hannah was finished, he straightened up and took his cell phone from off his belt. Angus studied the contact list and made a call. It was a call which would change the lives of all three people standing by the wall.

Angus looked at Mary Elizabeth. He had not really taken a good look at her before, but it was obvious that her encounter with Hannah had changed her. She looked softer to him than when they had visited in his office, and there was no doubting the concerned for someone else that owned her face. His gaze also took in Hannah, her face streaked with tears but nonetheless a face that looked exactly like Mary Elizabeth.

He thought about his own situation. Thirty-three and divorced. No children and no significant other. After his wife left him, he had given up on women and pretended to like living alone. Looking at the two tearful people before him he suddenly realized that he was lonely just like the two of them were. He would do all he could to help bring the two of them together, and then he would see if there was a way he could fit in.

The social worker on call arrived a few minutes later, and she too heard Hannah and Mary Elizabeth's stories. She did not seem shocked at all but just nodded her head as she listened. It was a familiar story to her. When they were finished talking the HRS agent told Hannah to get in the back seat of her car.

She looked at Mary Elizabeth and spoke, "You can follow me to the office if you like. I will have to put Hannah in temporary custody in a safe place. I will be happy to put your case before the juvenile judge for consideration of permanent custody. I'm not sure how that will work out, though."

In the weeks that followed, Angus saw more of Mary Elizabeth than any of his other parolees. He knew he was becoming involved and attached but couldn't stop himself. Finally, he went to his supervisor and requested to have Mary Elizabeth transferred to another patrol officer. Angus pointed out that Mary Elizabeth only had three months left before she would be a free person.

When his supervisor heard the reason, he shook his head. "Not a good idea, Officer Cauthen, not a good idea at all."

In spite of that warning, the transfer was made, and Angus went to Mary Elizabeth's workplace and told her. He also asked her to go to supper with him that night. She said yes.

A whirlwind romance ensued as two lonely people found comfort and love in each other's company. The two of them found they had many things in common and one of the greatest of these was a desire to have Hannah out of foster care and in a real home. The social worker arranged for Mary Elizabeth to visit Hannah and those visits quickly bridged the gap of a lost decade.

The Johnsons were brought to trial and based on the taped testimony of Hannah were convicted of child abuse and sexual abuse, and the judge added that he wished they could be tried for the death of Billy Willis. The judge felt sure they were guilty even if they did not actually take the child's life with their own hands. It was no surprise that he gave them the maximum sentence allowed by law.

Hannah did well in her new foster home, not only because the family was kind and loving but because she now had hope of having a real home with her own mother. She had quickly fallen in love with Angus who felt the same way about her. The court, however, seemed reluctant to move in favor of giving Mary Elizabeth custody.

Mary Elizabeth blossomed. Her personality underwent a complete one hundred, and eighty degree turn around. Part of it was due to courtship with Angus, but the majority came from the love rekindled by having Hannah in her life. The desire to be with Hannah grew with every visit. Mary Elizabeth got the new job she had wanted and then a long-awaited moment came. Her five year probation period finally ended.

Angus and Hannah joined her for a major celebration. They went to Mary Elizabeth's favorite Italian restaurant, and Angus ordered gelato for dessert. Then he handed her a small black box, a special gift, he said. Mary Elizabeth's eyes went wide when she opened it, and then they filled with tears.

"Will you?" Angus asked.

"Oh, Yes," was the answer.

All eyes were on the bride and groom in the simple ceremony held in the judge's office, and so they missed the happiest face which happened to be standing next to the bride. Just before the vows began, the judge had whispered in Hannah's ear.

"When they return from their honeymoon, I'm placing you in the custody of your mother."

And so, **"Weeping may tarry for the night...*but joy comes with the morning*. (Psalm 30:5)"**

THE END

Wanda

by Philip Dampier

(This story is based on a prompt suggested by the author Steven King)

Chapter 1

Arvie Anderson left his small but neat office at five after five on the first Monday after the first of the year. He wasn't expected anywhere special, so he decided to stop at a small bar on his way to the apartment he shared with Scratch, his large gray cat.

He found Scratch when he was a senior in college. The kitten had been abandoned, and Arvie's soft heart couldn't bear to leave it in the cold. Scratch was now his best friend. They had learned each other's personal habits and had developed a live and let live relationship. Scratch was well fed and medically sound. He loved to curl up next to Arvie during television time, and Arvie would scratch his ears, absentmindedly, as he watched whatever show was on. People don't actually own cats, but Scratch seemed to think he owned Arvie.

There had been an occasional girlfriend, but nothing lasting had developed. Arvie wasn't feeling any particular need, but he was open to a relationship with the opposite sex if the right one presented itself. Scratch could care less. Whenever a female visited the apartment, Scratch usually made himself scarce. He was a one-person cat and was aloof to anyone else.

Arvie stopped at the Campus Pub at least once a week because it was near the university campus where he had graduated, and he sometimes saw some of his old classmates there. He had graduated from the university two years earlier with a degree in computer engineering and management.

Visiting the bar was a way of keeping in touch with the academic community he thought, and it was better than being alone the whole time. He would have a beer or two, gossip a bit if friends were there and then go home to check on Scratch and fix them both some supper.

The small neighborhood bar wasn't particularly dark, the neon lights just bright enough to cast shadows and illuminate faces. He sat down on a bar stool and looked around. No one he knew, but then it was early. The TV on the wall behind the bar was showing pictures of Jack Kennedy and discussing his upcoming inauguration. He wasn't big in politics, but he watched the story while he sipped his beer. He sat where he could see the entrance in the large mirror behind the bar in case someone he knew came in.

He was on his second O'Doul's when a group of students burst through the doors with noisy chattering, as college students often did. He looked them over for a familiar face but halfway through the group his eyes stopped. The girl stood out like an evergreen in a winter hardwood forest. Tall, dark-haired, fair complexion, and something else. She had a sexy aura around her. Hard to explain but he felt it. She was dressed in typical campus style, shorts and a tee with Nikes. But the sex appeal was there. He felt it across the room.

Their eyes locked. She took in his blond hair and black-rimmed glasses. She smiled. He smiled back. She stepped away from her group and advanced towards him.

"Is this stool taken?"

"No, it's not. Please sit down."

He watched her climb on the stool; small purse clutched in her hand. His heart stopped beating for a few seconds, and his brain went slack to the action at hand. When everything caught up, he managed to speak.

"I'm Arvie Anderson." It was an effort, but he managed to get it out in a clear voice. He wasn't sure if he should offer his hand or not.

"Wanda Williams," she responded, "nice to meet you." Wanda stuck out her hand. Arvie took hold of it and gave a polite shake or two. When their hands touched, he felt an electric current run up his arm. It was very disconcerting. He could just smell her perfume, not strong but a different scent. He wasn't sure what it smelled like, but it seemed to fit her somehow.

"Nice to meet you. May I buy you a beer or something else to drink?" he asked.

"Bud Lite, please and thank you."

Small talk began and the minutes turned into an hour. Arvie glanced at his watch and realized he had not fed the cat and he hadn't had supper.

"Wanda, I'm starved. Would you like to have a bite to eat with me?"

Her smile devastated him at the same time her answer sent shivers through his body.

"Why thank you, Arvie, I'd be delighted to dine with you."

Arvie paid the bar tab and escorted his new lady friend to the door. He knew a quiet restaurant just a few blocks up the street, and he motioned for her to accompany him. They weren't really dressed for dining out, but neither of them seemed to care.

Beer at the bar and then supper at a small dinner nearby became the pattern for the rest of the week. They spent the weekend with each other, and a whirlwind romance ensued. Arvie found himself unable to think about anything but Wanda. She interrupted his sleep by appearing in his dreams, and she took away his concentration when he tried to focus at work.

He neglected his cat that had been his constant companion every evening for the past four years. It was suddenly impossible to function outside of his fixation on Wanda. He felt sure she had the same experience. He felt it, not because she told him so but he also could feel it by the way that she looked at him and touched him.

He would naturally move with caution in a new relationship being somewhat shy and introverted. She was the exact opposite. She seemed eager to hurry the pace and move from friends to lovers to… could he dare think it, engagement?

After a month Arvie knew she was not only sexy but extremely smart. Her major was in biochemistry, and she was on the Dean's List. She happily took the lead role in their relationship, and he felt powerless to intervene even if he wanted to, but he didn't want to at the time.

Little by little she took control of their interactions. Arvie didn't think anything about her choosing the restaurants, or suggesting the movies they attended. She began to suggest what he should wear when they went out, and he happily agreed. Arvie wanted to please her, and he never thought about the fact that the relationship had shifted from his control to hers. He was snowed, completely. He was ten feet under without a shovel and didn't realize it.

Before he knew what had happened, he had proposed, and a date had been set, and a wedding was planned. She informed him he would have to move out of his apartment as she wouldn't live there under any circumstances. She found a new place that suited her better, and he severed his lease and made arrangements to move. It was then the first bombshell fell.

"Don't you just love the new apartment?" Wanda asked.

"Yes, it's very nice, much roomier than my old one. I think I will go ahead and move my things in so I can get the old apartment cleaned up."

"Good idea."

"I think Scratch will adjust to new dwellings very well."

"Arvie, you're not bringing that cat to the new apartment."

"What?"

"I said you aren't bringing Scratch to our new apartment. I don't like cats."

"You never mentioned this to me before. I've had Scratch for four years now. He's like part of my family."

"Well, you're getting a new family. A family without smelly, hair producing animals. I am not having it in my house."

Arvie just stood there. He was dumbfounded and felt like he had been blindsided by a defensive end.

Wanda moved closer to him, putting her arms around his shoulders and her lips next to his ear. He could smell the intoxicating fumes of her perfume that had become a part of her body, her person, it seemed.

"Don't fret, Arvie. I'll make you forget Scratch. Believe me, and I'm all the cat you're ever going to need."

The wedding went exactly as Wanda planned it. They spent five days in Mexico on their honeymoon before taking joint possession of the apartment. The apartment was now completely furnished, the décor and furnishings all of Wanda's choosing. Arvie had found Scratch a good home, but in the back of his mind, a small coal of resentment was warming. Things went along well for about a week. That was when Arvie decided to take the garbage out.

"What do you think you're doing?" Wanda asked.

Arvie just looked at her, kitchen garbage bag in his left hand, right hand holding onto the doorknob.

"I'm taking this smelly garbage out to the dumpster."

"Put it back!"

"Why? It smells, and I need to stretch my legs."

"Put it back and don't touch it again. I'll take it out when I'm ready to take it out. This is my house. Nothing goes out, and nothing comes in unless I say so. Do you understand me?"

Arvie just stood there, unable to speak. The cat coal in the back of his mind gained a degree or two of heat. He walked back to the kitchen and put the garbage bag back in the container. Without speaking, he walked out of the room into the den and turned on the TV. This was the first time he acknowledged to himself that his new wife was more than smart and sexy. She came into the room and took a chair opposite him, holding a large wine glass in her hand.

"Wanda, how many glasses of wine is that?

"Are you counting?"

"Someone needs too."

"I can handle my wine and how many glasses I drink in the evening is none of your damn business."

Arvie looked at her. She looked back. He saw her in a different light than he had ever seen her before and it scared him. His father had been an alcoholic, and he had seen as well as felt the turmoil and storm it brought to his childhood home.

"My dad drank too much. Seeing you drinking like this is disturbing. It brings back bad memories."

"I'm not your dad, and I'm not an alcoholic, Arvie. I just like a little wine before bedtime."

"I understand, sweetheart, but a little grows into more and more and…"

"Shut up about it. You drink what you want, and I'll drink what I want."

The conversation ended. Arvie turned his attention to the TV and the news network. During the commercials, he cast a side glance her way. It seemed her glass was always full. Before they went to bed, Arvie counted at least four glasses. Arvie didn't sleep too well that night. It wouldn't be the last time that happened.

Chapter 2

Two months later Arvie came home thirty minutes later than his normal time. He keyed his apartment door and stepped inside.

"Hi Honey, I'm home."

Wanda came from the kitchen into the entryway, wine glass in hand.

"Where have you been; you're thirty minutes late."

"I stopped by our bar and had a beer with an old friend."

"Who was she?"

"Not she, he. He was Wally Johnson. We were in the same fraternity when I was at State."

"I'll just bet it was an old fraternity brother. You're flirting around with another woman, aren't you?."

"No, Wanda. The only woman in my life is you."

"Well, you're supper is cold. Help yourself. I'm going to the den and finish this bottle of wine."

"Wanda, please don't do that. You're drinking way too much. It's making you cross."

Wanda turned around and glared at him while she took a long and slow deliberate swallow of wine.

"You're a nerd Arvie. Don't want to have fun and don't want anyone else to. What in the world did I ever see in you?"

Week by week the tension between Arvie and Wanda grew tighter. Her drinking increased and with it her accusations against him. She began to suggest that he had a mistress or that he was gay. She accused him of not wanting to have sex with her. She laughed when he pointed out that she was drunk almost every night when they went to bed and was in no shape to have sex with anyone.

Within six months Arvie was thinking about divorce. He tried over and over to reason with Wanda to no avail. One Saturday before the drinking grew even worse he took her for a walk in the small tree-filled park just a few blocks from their apartment. After thirty minutes of strolling, he stopped her at a green, wooden bench and took a seat. She leaned back and stared at the clouds.

"Wanda?"

"Yes."

"I can't go on this way. The way we're living. Something has to give. Either you stop the drinking, or I'm moving out and getting a place of my own. I'll file for a divorce; you won't have to do anything."

Wanda didn't move nor did she respond for several minutes. She just kept staring at the sky as if he had never spoken. Finally, she dropped her head and turned it towards him. Tears were in her eyes.

"I'm sorry, Arvie. I've been a bitch, I know. We need something to hold us together. If I stop drinking will you agree to stay and let us have a baby?"

Arvie thought it over. He loved Wanda, but he was frustrated. Probably frustrated the most at himself because he had been such a wimp in their marriage and hadn't taken control as he should have. A small voice was trying to tell him that he didn't know who he was dealing with. Something was amiss, but he wanted things to be right so much that he squelched any negative thoughts.

"Yes. I would like to do that."

Wanda eased off the wine and then stopped altogether. Things improved although she still called the shots. Arvie came in from work one Friday with plans for them for the weekend.

"Hey Honey, I've got tickets to a concert at the Arena."

"That's great but not the greatest. I have the greatest."

"Oh, really? I don't think so. I've got tickets to the Rolling Stones concert tomorrow night. Great seats."

"Oh, really? I'm going to have a baby."

"Oh, really? That's wonderful. I'm so excited.   Let's celebrate by going to the Rolling Stones concert."

He grabbed her and put his arms around her. It was a magical moment, and for a while, it seemed like things were as they were in the beginning. Wanda struggled through the pregnancy with bouts of sickness and depression, but somehow she managed not to indulge in wine. To help, Arvie removed all that was in the house and made sure none was brought back in. He gave up his trips to the college tavern, willing to forego a beer if it would help Wanda stay sober.

Six months and three days later, Jill was born. She was beautiful, just like her mother. Wanda worked at being a good mother, but it was a struggle for her. She was jealous of the relationship of Arvie and Jill. She was also jealous of the time that Jill took. She was so used to being her own boss, and she hated the demands made on her by an infant and then a small child. Arvie was oblivious to the slow change in her as Jill grew older. He was now in a paradise of his own creation, and Jill furnished the rose-colored lenses he saw his small private world through. A day of reckoning was coming. It was just a matter of time.

Chapter 3

They celebrated Jill's third birthday with a private party. For all of her three years, things had been up and down in her family. Her dad worshipped the ground she walked on, and she had him wrapped around her finger. She loved her mother as well, but things were different with her. The mother wasn't wrapped around anyone's finger. Jill soon learned that no crying or fit throwing or loving persuasion had any effect on her mother. She also was aware that her mother was in charge of her dad as well.

Still, things weren't too bad, until one day her mom took her to a luncheon with one of her friends. Jill knew her mom was drinking something besides water or soda, but she had no idea what it was. Nor was she aware of the purchase her mother made at the small store down the street from their house on the way home.

Wanda sent Jill off to play, she stayed in the kitchen, a glass and a bottle on the table. In the trash was an empty one, finished an hour earlier. Wanda ignored Jill but Jill was having fun playing with her toys, and she knew her daddy would be home soon. The house was quiet and peaceful. Jill moved from plaything to plaything, finally deciding she would ride the beautiful hobby horse her dad had given her on her third birthday.

The trouble began when her dad came home.

Arvie opened the door and walked in. He was almost an hour late. He had called earlier, but the phone was never picked up. Jill was riding her hobby horse in the den, he could hear the springs as she bounced up and down, but he didn't see or hear Wanda.

"Wanda?"

She came out of the kitchen, wine glass in one hand and a knife in another. Her eyes were red, and she looked like a wild person. She threw her head back and laughed.

"So, the little skirt chaser finally made it home. How was she today, you loser?"

"Oh no, Wanda, please put the wine up and the knife down. I had to work late. I tried to call you, but you didn't answer."

"Ha, sure you did. I'm tired of your running around on me, and I'm going to stop it now."

She lunged towards him with the butcher knife cutting an arc towards his face. Arvie was barely able to duck the swing. What really saved him was she was so intoxicated that her reflexes were slow and her body unstable.

Arvie ran through the den scooping up Jill as he did so. He entered their bedroom and locked the door behind him, his breathing labored. Jill squealed.

"Oh, Daddy. Run with me like that again. That was fun."

Arvie ignored her for the moment, reaching for the phone on the bedside table and punching the zero.

"Give me the police, please. Emergency. Hurry."

The phone rang and rang. Wanda was pounding on the bedroom door and screaming his name amid obscenities.

"This is the city police; how can I help you?"

116

"This is Arvie Anderson, and I live at 225 Rose Avenue, Apartment 7. My wife is drunk and threatening me with a large knife. She actually tried to stab me. I have a three-year-old daughter and she and I are locked in the bedroom. Please hurry. I don't know what she might do."

Ten minutes later the police were pounding on the front door of the apartment. They were met by a drunken woman with a large knife in her hands. A scuffle ensued, and Wanda was taken into custody. Arvie unlocked the door and brought a very frightened Jill out with him. The officers took his statement and asked if he wanted to file charges.

"I want her away from my daughter and me. I want some kind of a restraining order against her."

"Fine, we'll take her in and let her sober up. She'll be in detox overnight. You follow us down, and we'll start the paperwork."

Later, after the paperwork was completed, Arvie called a locksmith and had the front door lock changed. Even if Wanda was in detox, he didn't feel safe. He was afraid for himself, but he was more afraid for Jill. What was this doing to her? He could tell that she was in a state of shock. He held her close and read her favorite books to her. She wanted to sleep with him, and he agreed. He wanted her in his room, too.

Arvie felt like he was in a nightmare that had no end. Jill went to sleep cuddled up next to him, her favorite bear beside her. Arvie didn't appear to sleep at all. He thought he might have slept a few minutes at a time but not longer.

When the night was finally over, he got up and made breakfast. He made a couple of calls. One was to Jill's daycare to explain that she would no longer be going there. He then called another place further away from their apartment. He was relieved that they had an opening. He tried to explain the situation to the lady who took his call, but he found it very difficult.

"It's all right Mr. Anderson. We understand. Yours is not an unusual request. Rest assured that no one will be allowed to pick up your daughter but you."

"Thank you. That is a relief. As I said, the police have her mother in custody right now, but she will be released today after she sobers up. They promised to give her the restraint order before letting her go, but they don't know her like I do. She will try to get Jill and then she will use Jill to get to me. I'm so afraid that Jill will get hurt."

"Don't you worry, sir. We'll take care of Jill. Everything will work out I'm sure."

Sometime that morning the restraint order was issued. Arvie took Jill to the new daycare center and stayed long enough to assure her and him that she would be alright. He kissed her several times before finally closing the door. From the center, he went to work. He wasn't sure what he could get done and thought about asking for the day off. Then he decided he was as safe there as anywhere and he needed to do something to get his mind off Wanda and her attack. He didn't understand what had caused the drinking or the violence. Five minutes after he sat down at his desk his extension phone rang.

"Anderson."

"You sorry, feeble excuse for a man. Where have you hidden my daughter and why did you change the locks to my apartment?"

"Wanda. It's over between us. You have a restraining order. You will not see our daughter or me until a judge says so and I hope that is a long time. Don't call me again."

Arvie hung up the phone but didn't return to his work. He just sat there and stared at the phone. He didn't really know what to do. Would she go get drunk? Did she have money? She had her card to his account, what should he do about that? She could clean out their account. He reached for the phone again. This time it was him calling the bank. After a long conversation with someone at the bank office, he knew he had to go to the bank and set up new accounts. He looked to see if his boss was busy so he could ask for a few minutes to go downstairs to his bank's branch in his own building.

He stood up on his way to see his boss when the phone rang again. Arvie answered it and then abruptly hung up. Arvie moved out his office door and across the hall to his supervisor's desk. He explained that he had an emergency at the bank and needed to go downstairs.

"Not a problem, just let me know when you're back, okay?"

"Sure, thanks, Ralph."

"Hey, isn't that your phone ringing? Seems like its rung a lot this morning."

"I'll take care of it."

Arvie called the police. They had released Wanda after she sobered up and was served the warrant. They had no idea where she was.

"Look, Mr. Anderson, usually these things work out as soon as the person is sober. She'll be all rosy dozy before you get home from work."

"I don't think so. What if she gets drunk again? I don't want to go through this night after night. I'm afraid to let her around my daughter."

"I suggest you call a lawyer but in the meantime, if something happens just call us and we'll be right out to take care of it."

Arvie hung up the phone and went downstairs to the bank. He spoke to a lady at a customer service desk to explain what he wanted to do but not much as to why. She led him into a small office where he was introduced to a young banker. It took twenty minutes and several sheets of paper, but he left with a new account and some new counter checks. The old accounts were closed, and a large amount of funds had been placed in the new checking account for the time being. Arvie wasn't sure what he would need to do if things got worse.

Arvie and two of his co-workers decided to go out to lunch together. They had been friends since Arvie joined the company and often had lunch at a nearby restaurant. Arvie told them about the previous night's events. They were both in disbelief at his story, but they could see the strain on Arvie's face.

They picked a large restaurant two blocks away which had seating outside in an area bordered by a low fence. Halfway through his salad, Arvie heard a disturbance. He turned towards the outside entrance in time to see Wanda come through the door. Her hair was disheveled and her clothes rumpled. Her gait was as unsteady as it was purposeful. She was weaving in a direct line towards Arvie. The knife in her right hand was large and new. The words coming out of her mouth were laced with obscenities, and spit was drooling from the left side of the corner of her mouth.

Chairs flew, and tables turned over as people hurried to get out of her way. Arvie stood up, the table situated between the two of them. Wanda screamed like a wild person and tried to strike him across the top of the table. Again and again, she slashed at him as they moved in a circle, the table between them. The sound of Pounding feet reached his ears, and two policemen jumped the small fence separating the dining area from the sidewalk.

They grabbed the knife and wrestled Wanda to the cement floor. More police arrived, and soon Wanda was cuffed and somewhat dragged over to a waiting van, all the time screaming at Arvie and struggling against her captors every step of the way.

Fright overcame Arvie, and his nerves gave way to the fear. He was instantly concerned about Jill and the apartment. His co-workers just looked at him. Neither of them knew what to say.

"I'm not going back to work guys, I've got to take care of some things," Arvie said.

"Are you all right?" one of them asked, "Don't you think you ought to go someplace and lie down?"

"No, not now. I have to find a place for Jill and me. I can't go through this every day."

"My God, man. This's awful. We'll talk to Ralph. Don't worry; he'll be supportive," the co-worker said.

"Right, Arvie. Can we help in any other way?" the second co-worker asked.

"No, thank you. I need to find a new place for the two us where we can be safe. I hope they lock her up this time," Arvie answered.

Chapter 4

The old house stood on a narrow lot right on the corner where the city bus stopped. There was no front entrance, it had been closed off years before and the steps to the porch removed. The porch had been walled up for three feet and then screened to the roof. A sidewalk ran up to it but now where the steps had been there were waist high shrubs.

There were two other entrances, one off the back porch which led into the kitchen and the dining room, the other from the kitchen to the backyard. There was a living room, one bath, and two bedrooms. There was an attic with regular stairs coming down into the small bedroom near the dining room and a basement where the gravity fed furnace sat. The door to the basement was next to a backyard door on the backside of the kitchen. They were asking ten thousand dollars for the property, and Arvie rented it immediately with the intent to buy once things settled down.

His next step was to call the police to learn about Wanda. He found out she was in a psychiatric ward under heavy sedation. The detective he spoke with assured him she would be transferred to a forensic psychiatric hospital as soon as the judge looked at the case.

He hired local transit people to move his furniture. The house was just what he wanted. It was cozy, near a park and out of the way. Wanda was locked up; at last, he felt he could relax.

Jill was okay with her new daycare site, but she didn't adjust well to the house even though it had a backyard with a swing set already installed. Arvie thought it might not be the house as much as it was the absence of Wanda. The first night she cried and asked to be in his room. He wasn't sure what to do. He tried to talk to her about the new house and how safe it was for them.

"My room is too far away from you," she said.

"No honey, there are just two rooms between us. I can hear you, and you can hear me."

"I hear noises upstairs."

"We don't have an upstairs. Oh, you mean the attic." Arvie was sorry now that he had shown her the huge attic. He thought it might make a great playroom later when he could fix it up.

"The noise you hear is just the wind. How about if daddy puts the stereo in your room and plays music for you when you go to sleep."

"I don't like it here, and I want Mommy."

"I know you do, sweetheart but Mommy is sick and in the hospital. When she's all well, we can see her again."

This same discussion occupied every night for the first week they were there. He finally gave in and bought a small bed which he put in the large bedroom with him. This seemed to solve the bed problem but not the Mommy problem. He didn't know what to do about the Mommy problem.

Would Wanda ever get well? He had been to the forensic hospital twice to talk to a psychiatrist but could get little assurance of anything. Evidently, they were keeping Wanda sedated as she was still very aggressive. For that reason, they wouldn't let him see her. He had guilt feelings about that, but in a way, it was a relief.

He and Jill went to the park a few blocks down the street on Saturday. It had lots of swings and other playground equipment as well as shaded picnic areas complete with grills. Sunday, they returned with picnic supplies and enjoyed a wonderful afternoon.

While they were in the park, a young woman with a daughter close to Jill's age came over to them and introduced herself. The little girl's name was Frannie, and she and Jill became quick friends. The mother also had a nice red dog she brought with them, and the girls played on the grass area with the dog chasing and jumping on them. Arvie asked about the dog, thinking maybe having one would help Jill not be so lonely.

He and the young mother, Martha Smith, exchanged addresses. He also got her phone number so they could arrange play dates for the girls. He told her he would call her as soon as he could get a phone installed. They agreed to meet at the park the next Saturday and have lunch together.

Martha Smith kept one eye on Franny and with the other watched Arvie and Jill walk to their car. He was a nice looking man she thought. She wondered about his wife. He actually hadn't mentioned her. Of course, she hadn't mentioned her ex either.

Maybe he wasn't married. Wouldn't that be something? He had been pleasant to talk to, and she was feeling lonely. She hadn't been on a date in quite some time, and she missed male companionship. The time had really flown by while they had been talking. She allowed herself to dream a little.

Five days later Arvie went home early from work. The phone company asked him to meet them at the house so they could install his new phone. The waiting list had been very long, and he didn't want to miss his turn. It was his plan to rest while he waited on the installer and then pick Jill up and the two of them go get pizza together. That was the latest thing she had learned at daycare. Once a week they had pizza, and it was all she wanted to eat now.

Arvie entered the house and went into the living room. He had picked up a newspaper at the bus stop on his way home and put it in his bag. He just wanted to sit in his new comfortable chair and work the crossword puzzle. He had just bought a new leather recliner, and he plopped down and looked out the window. He could swivel and see the door to Jill's bedroom or even further into the edge of the kitchen. He could also see out the side window of the living room. He preferred looking out at the hedge and trees in the front yard, so he pivoted the chair that way. Occasionally a neighbor would walk by after getting off the bus. He planned on trying to meet some of them in the days ahead.

As he gazed out the panes of glass, he realized that something was wrong, but he couldn't quite figure out what it was. The house had an odd smell. It was a pleasant odor that was light and somewhat vague. He knew it was foreign to the house but not his nose. It was just strong enough for him to identify it as an odor. He got up and walked into the kitchen but didn't see where he had left anything out. He opened the fridge and got out a soda and took it back to his seat in the living room.

He unfolded the newspaper to turn to the puzzle when his eyes caught a small headline halfway down the page.

"TWO PATIENTS ESCAPE LOCAL FORENSIC HOSPITAL, NURSE SERIOUSLY WOUNDED"

He scanned the article, but no names were given. Both of the escapees were women. A chill went down his spine, and his body temperature seemed as if it dropped several degrees. He realized that the scent he had smelled earlier was growing stronger. His brain cleared, and he knew what it was. It was Wanda's perfume.

He started to get up from his chair, but he froze as he heard footfalls on the stairs leading down from the attic to Jill's bedroom. He looked around for the phone and remembered it hadn't been installed yet. He knew without looking that it was Wanda and he also knew that she would have her favorite kitchen utensil in her hand.

He wanted to jump up and run, but at first, his legs wouldn't work. The door to the attic closed with a quiet click. The perfume was strong in his nose and brain now. He reached down to release the handle of the recliner, the newspaper and pencil dropping onto the floor. He saw the door from the bedroom open. It was Wanda. She wasn't drunk, and she wasn't screaming. She was smiling.

"You've been a bad boy, Arvie. Mommy's got to punish you."

Not only were Arvie's feet and hands frozen but his tongue was as well. He just stared. The knife was by her side, but as she moved towards him, it began to rise in slow motion. In fact, it seemed to Arvie that everything was moving in slow motion.

Wanda was still smiling as the distance between them narrowed. Three feet away and the knife was over her head, hand extended for the greatest force.

There was a loud knock on the door, and a voice called out."

"Phone Company, Mr. Alexander."

It was as if an electric shock hit Arvie. He jumped to his feet just as the knife descended towards him. It missed his arm by a fraction of an inch and pierced the back of the recliner about where his heart had been. The lunge threw Wanda off balance, and she fell to the floor. Arvie never looked back but ran to the door. He threw it opened and threw his arms around a startled Bell installer.

"Thank God. Call the police at once and shut the door."

For a moment the coveralled installer stood still in shock. He disengaged himself from Arvie's impromptu hug and pushed the door shut. They heard a ripping sound and a loud shriek. The shriek was followed by a loud thump as something heavy hit the floor. Arvie tried to pull the installer down the steps, but the installer was trying to look inside the window beside him on the porch. Arvie let go his arm and started down the steps.

The door flew open, and Wanda busted through it, knife in hand and a banshee cry on her lips. It was then that the installer thought to run, but it was too late. He turned and stepped on the first step just as Wanda reached him with the knife. She swung it right at his throat and cut through the skin to the jugular. Blood flew, spraying on the post holding the porch roof up, then running down to the steps.

Arvie had made it to the bottom step when he tripped and fell out onto the grass. He rolled over in time to see Wanda swing at the unfortunate phone installer. He began to crawl across the lawn in an effort to get to his feet and run. Wanda was hampered by the body of the phone man, and when she finally moved it out of the way, Arvie was on his feet and moving across the yard to the house directly behind his.

He could run faster than her, and he did. He headed for the neighboring house hoping to get inside. Most of his neighbors didn't lock their doors, and he hoped the McClain's, the one set of neighbors he had met had not locked theirs. He was also hoping Mrs. McClain didn't work and he could lock the door and use the phone. He had only talked to them once, but they seemed like nice people.

Arvie easily outdistanced Wanda and gained the front porch and the door to the neighbor's house. But Wanda did not pursue him. Instead, she ran to the corner of the McClain house where the phone line entered at the foundation and attacked the wire leading into the house with her large knife. With a sinister grin, she walked unhurriedly to the back door.

Arvie pounded on the door and pushed it open. He spun around and turned the lock lever. Mrs. McClain stepped into the living room from the door into the kitchen. She stopped in the middle of the room when she saw Arvie. He looked pale and out of breath. She looked startled.

"Why Mr. Alexander. It is Alexander, isn't it? What on earth is wrong?

"Need your phone, emergency. Please lock your back door."

"What…"

"Hurry, ma'am. Lock the door."

Mrs. McClain went to the door not understanding but willing to obey. Just as she reached the door, it swung open propelled by a mania induced strength.

That fact actually saved her life. The blow of the door was so strong that it threw her against the wall and her body was hidden by the door itself. It also helped that Arvie was standing right in the line of sight of Wanda who had flung the door open, and now stood there smiling at him once more.

"Well, Arvie, you idiot of a man, we meet again. Locked yourself in haven't you?"

Arvie backed towards the door. His hand found the handle. His fingers searched for the lock itself.

"If you open the door Arvie, I will have to hurt you in the back. Wouldn't you rather face me?"

"Why are you doing this, Wanda? What is wrong with you?"

"Why nothing is wrong with me, Arvie. You know that you're the problem. Always have been, haven't you? Always wanting to take over and be the boss. Trying to sneak my things out of the house in the garbage. Trying to bring things in without me knowing it."

"Wanda, I never did either of those things. You took care of the garbage, and you checked every bag I brought in."

"Don't try to kid me, Arvie. I know what you were doing. Stopping by that bar to meet those college girls."

"I never met any girls, college or not. I never had any woman but you."

"Ha, that's funny. You thought I was blind, didn't you? Then you stole my daughter. Those college girls weren't enough for you. You had to have Jill too. You fixed it so that she always wanted to be with you. She was crazy about you, and you were crazy about her. You forgot me, didn't you? College girls and Jill, that was your life. I was squeezed out."

"Wanda, that's ridiculous. Jill loves you. You lost touch because of the wine. You missed her affection because you were drunk half the time. You missed both of our affection because of the wine."

"You'd like me to believe that, but I know better. But it's over. I'm going to get rid of you and take Jill back with me, and she'll forget all about you." Wanda moved towards Arvie as she spoke.

Wanda's raised her arm, the knife reflecting the ceiling light, and a sneer crossed her face. Arvie had no more room to retreat. His eyes grew big as he looked past Wanda.

While all the conversation was going on between Arvie and Wanda, Mrs. McClain was recovering from the blow of the opening door. She pushed the door back without allowing it to shut.

Her first thought was to run. She had never been so frightened in her life. She knew if she did run she would never get the look on Mr. Anderson's face out of her mind. She wasn't a brave woman, but she had a heart.

She looked around her for something she could use as a weapon. What she saw was her mother's cast iron skillet sitting on the top of the stove. It really belonged in the pull out tray at the bottom of the range, but it was so heavy she often just left it on the stove top.

She moved from behind the door to the side of the range and picked up the large frying pan. It took both hands to lift it over her head. She moved towards the knife yielding woman as quietly as she could, but in reality, it didn't matter. Wanda wasn't listening; she was talking. Wanda only had one thing in mind, lucky for Mrs. McClain and Arvie, too.

When the iron skillet hit the back of Wanda's head the knife she had been holding flew across space and landed point-in the door just above Arvie's hand. Wanda landed on the floor, breathing but not conscious.

"Oh, my God," Mrs. McClain exclaimed, "I've killed her."

Arvie bent down and checked Wanda's pulse.

"No, you haven't, but I wish you had. Where is your phone?"

"Right here, on the wall by the stove."

Arvie picked it up and then put it back down.

"She's cut the line. Who else has a phone?"

"This way," Mrs. McClain headed for the back door.

Arvie was right behind her. Wanda and the skillet were on the floor. The knife was stuck in the door. Later, Arvie wondered why he didn't take the knife with him.

The two of them headed across the McClain's grass and into a neighboring backyard at a quick pace. Mrs. McClain was alternating rubbing her hands together and rubbing them in her hair.

When they arrived at the neighbor's back door, Mrs. McClain knocked and called out loud.

"Joanna, Joanna, come quick. Let us in."

An older woman opened the door and looked at them. She had a paring knife in her left hand and an apple in the other.

"Come in Doris, what's the matter? Who is this? I was just about to fix an apple pie."

"Excuse me, Ma'am," Arvie spoke up, "we need to use your phone. We have to call the police."

When everyone was inside, Joanna showed Arvie the phone on the kitchen wall, and while he was dialing, Doris began to explain the awful events of the past few minutes. The realization of what had happened just dawning in her head. She felt faint, and Joanna went back to the kitchen to get her a glass of water. She was just in time to listen in on Arvie's conversation with the police.

"Yes, the same woman. She's knocked out at the house behind mine."

"I'm 1462 Chestnut Drive. She's in the McClain house behind it. Hurry before she wakes up."

"You better send an ambulance to my house because I think she may have seriously hurt the phone man who was there to install my phone.

"No, I was running away, and I don't know what happened, but if he was okay, he would have called you."

Arvie turned to Joanna, "Ma'am, can you tell me your address?"

Joanna gave him the number and street.

"Yes, officer. It's 1230 Walnut Lane. It's right behind the McClain house. Their backyards touch."

"Yes sir, we'll wait right here. "

"Don't worry; we'll lock the door."

Chapter 5

Wanda struggled to gain consciousness. Her head pounded where the skillet had hit her, and her heart raced from the excitement. She could feel the rage rebuilding in her body. She pushed up off of the floor, staggering but gathering her balance as she held to the stuffed chair near where she had fallen. Her eyes focused. The first thing she saw was her knife. It was still with her, in the house, stuck in the door.

Memory returned, she looked around, but the house was empty. What had hit her? She shook her head. She had to get out of there. She knew that. She needed to leave before those people in the white coats came and found her. She grabbed the knife and pulled it out of the door. It left a telling scar.

She went out the front door and across the lawn the way she had come. She parted the peonies that separated the two yards and headed for the back door of Arvie's new house. She grunted as she stepped over the prostrate body of the telephone installer. Inside she made her way into the bedroom with the attic stairs. She moved up the stairs into the dimly lit space.

It was tall enough to walk in standing up and was half the size of the house. One window occupied the east end. It was dirty, but she could see out of it enough to make things out. Next to the window old furniture leaned against the wall. The cover of dust suggested that it had been stored there for many years. Two wooden chairs and a complete bedroom set were up against the window.

The bed frame was very tall and had posters on each side, taller yet. It leaned against the wall, the post bracketing the window. Close by was a small table, suitable to place at the end of the bed for quilts or to use in front of a sofa. Wanda lifted it up and placed it behind the bedstead. She crawled up on top of it and spread out. She could raise up and look out the window, but she was invisible from the other side. All anyone would see would be the bed frame and the legs of the table. She was tired. She pulled her knees up and folded her arms. She lay her head on her arms and closed her eyes.

Sirens startled her out of her sleep. She barely raised her head and peeked out of the lower part of the window framing. Two, no three police cars were on the street, their lights spinning and flashing. She also saw an ambulance just outside the two brick posts that guarded the entrance to the lot. Men in white and men in blue were running in various directions. She could hear their voices.

"Over here," one cried.

"Is he dead?"

"I'm not sure. He's bleeding bad, and he's not conscious....yes, he's breathing, but it's shallow. Get a medic over here."

Then she heard a different voice. A voice she recognized. A voice she despised, Arvie's voice.

"She was hiding in the attic when I came home and then she tried to stab me in the living room. I ran next door, and she followed me there. My neighbor, Mrs. McClain hit her with a frying pan and knocked her out, and the two of us ran to the house where you picked me up."

"Is that the phone installer they're treating on the porch?"

"Yes, that's him. I tried to get him to run but he wouldn't. I don't know why. I think he didn't understand that it was a crazy person in the house."

Wanda's eyes widened and then narrowed. That rat, she thought. Who's he calling crazy? I'll make him think crazy. A new voice entered the conversation.

"Mr. Anderson, I'm Captain Vaughn of the City Police Department. If you'll step over to my car, I would like to ask you a few questions. While we do that, the Sergeant and one of the patrolmen will search your house. Do we have your permission or do we need a warrant?"

"No, no. Go ahead. I think she's run off. I think she's looking for my daughter or for me."

"Where is your daughter, by-the-way?"

"She's at Rocking Horse Day Care Center on Oak Street."

"I see. Let's go to the car and let these men do their job, shall we?"

Wanda heard the door open, and the two men walk into the house. She pulled herself into the smallest ball she could possibly make. She forced herself to take slow, quiet breaths. The policemen moved from room to room. She could hear them opening and closing doors. She knew when they knelt and looked under the beds in Arvie's room. She heard the hangers sliding on the pipes in the closet as they searched behind the clothes. It would only be a minute before they were going to be in the room where the attic door was.

She knew they wouldn't find her. They wouldn't walk across the dark, dusty attic when they could see the walls so clearly. She felt invisible and at the same time powerful. She had a mission, and those two amateurs wouldn't get in her way. She was too smart for them and for that idiot of a man, Arvie, too. Especially for Arvie. He would have been lost without her guidance. Couldn't make a decision on his own. She started to smile and then remembered how much she hated him.

The door to the attic opened. The beam from a flashlight flicked across the ceiling and then onto the stairs. The old stairs groaned under the weight of the two men. The two officers had their weapons ready, she was sure. She thought about jumping up and saying boo just to see them wet their pants but instead she enjoyed the picture she visualized.

The two officers stood at the top of the stairs and moved their lights around the room taking in every square foot. The beams stopped on the bedroom furniture. One of them spoke.

"Look at that old bedstead. You ever see anything like it?"

"Yeah, in my great-grandmother's house."

"Bet it would look nice all cleaned and polished."

"Probably. Nothing up here. Let's get out of here, this dust is killing me."

One of the officers bent down and sent his beam under the bedstead. He moved it back and forth. Wanda froze. She quit breathing. Thirty seconds went by. The beam moved away, and the policemen moved as well. She could hear them going down the stairway. Then the door shut. She let out her breath and took a new one in.

Next, they checked out the small basement under the kitchen but were quickly back upstairs. She heard the back door open and then close. She didn't move nor did she look out the window. No need to look. She knew what was out there. She would rest again and wait. There was time, and now she knew where Jill was.

Arvie shook hands with Captain Vaughn and looked at the house. The two house searchers had come to the car and informed the captain that the house was empty, but Arvie was too shook up to go back in there. As long as Wanda was loose and armed, he wouldn't go back in the house. He had to find a motel, and he had to get Jill to a safe place. He had to make some plans. Maybe he needed to quit his job and move to another state. He had never been so afraid in his life.

Arvie drove to the daycare and picked up Jill. Then he drove to a motel on the main highway heading south and got a room for them. He called the police captain and reported his whereabouts.

"Have you found Wanda?" he asked.

"No, we have an APB out for her. In her present state of mind, she shouldn't be hard to find. Wherever she goes, she's sure to attract attention. We'll have her in custody before the day is over; I'm sure."

Wanda waited until the last car drove away. She allowed herself a small peek out the window. From her limited view, everyone was gone. She decided to wait just a few minutes more. She lay still and didn't even allow herself to hum. After a bit, she raised up and looked outside. Nothing. She slid back and got to her feet. She moved slowly so as not to disturb a loose board if there was one, in case someone was hiding in the house besides her.

She maintained her caution going down the stairs, one hand on the wall and the other tightened around the large knife. She liked the large knife, it was heavy and very sharp. Wanda walked through the house and down to the basement. Satisfied that the place was empty, she went back to Jill's room and found her daughter's hairbrush. In the bathroom, she brushed her hair and washed her face. Her clothes were all askew, and she tugged them into line. She had no makeup to put on, but she thought she looked presentable.

She laid her favorite knife on the kitchen counter and eased out the kitchen door onto the porch. She was moving at a steady pace that didn't attract any unusual attention. No one would see her, as the neighbors had heard about the day's events and all their doors were locked, and the window blinds pulled down. Wanda headed up the street walking on the sidewalk towards the junior high school just a few blocks away. She had so much energy that she was enjoying the walk.

She had been the original daycare finder, and so she knew where every one of the facilities on that side of town was located. It was a twenty-minute walk to Oak Street and the Rocking Horse Daycare Center.

She practiced smiling as she walked, preparing to act the perfect mother. She just wanted to pick her daughter up herself. Wouldn't that moron Arvie be surprised when he went to get Jill and found her gone? She stopped humming and started laughing. She was very attractive when she smiled.

A high mesh fence enclosed The Center, and Wanda opened the gate and made her way to the front door. She could hear squeals and laughter inside. She turned the doorknob and pushed the door in. A young girl, maybe twenty or so, stood in the front room. As Wanda entered the room, the worker looked up, and a question mark appeared on her face. She knew all the parents, and she didn't know this lady.

"May I help you?" she asked.

"Yes, I'm Mrs. Anderson. I've come to pick up my daughter, Jill. Her dad is busy and can't get her today."

"Oh. Just a moment Mrs. Anderson."

The young girl turned and disappeared into the next room, and Wanda heard voices. She stepped further into the room, and an older lady startled her when she walked in. She had a look on her face as if she was trying to hide what she was feeling. Wanda sensed that something was amiss. The lady stopped short when she realized that Wanda had wandered into the second room.

"Mrs. Anderson?"

"Yes, I want my daughter, please."

"You daughter isn't here, Mrs. Anderson. Her father picked her up almost an hour ago. I don't understand why you are here. Mr. Anderson told me that you were in the hospital and only he was to pick up Jill."

"What? You can see that I'm not in a hospital and Jill is my daughter. That butthead is trying to keep her away from me. And you're helping him, aren't you? The two of you are in coo-hoots, aren't you?"

"No, no, we're just following instructions. We're not trying to get in anybody's private business."

Wanda's face had completely changed. Gone was the look of a loving mother and in its place was a snarling, spitting wildcat. She stepped closer to the daycare lady and struck her across the face.

Turning she swept a lamp off a table. The woman screamed, and the lamp crashed. Doors banged, and children started crying. The front door opened and a mother in search of her child came in. The shock on her face turned to terror when Wanda slammed her out of the way as she headed for the exit.

Oh, how Wanda wished she had brought her knife. The idiots would've paid for their conspiracy. She entertained the thought that she might just get the knife and come back.

Wanda crossed Oak Street and headed a block away from the daycare where she turned on Walnut. She walked in a direction away from the daycare and Arvie's house.

She decided she would wait until dark and then return to the house on Chestnut and see if Arvie was home. She would get rid of him once and for all and claim her child.

Arvie and Jill were just about to leave the motel room for supper when the room phone rang. Arvie picked it up and held it tight to his ear.

"Hello."

"Mr. Anderson?"

"Yes, this he."

"This is Captain Vaughn with the city police department. We just received a call from the daycare center where your daughter was. Your wife was there looking for the girl. She attacked the owner and another person. We're scouring the neighborhood but haven't found her so far.

 I don't think you should take your daughter back there. In fact, the owner told me to tell you not to come back. I'm sorry. I think you should stay put until we find her."

"Oh my goodness. Please find her quick. She's crazy for sure."

"We'll find her. Don't worry."

Chapter Six

Meanwhile, Wanda decided to head towards the house with the attic. Darkness was falling, and she wanted to be off of the streets. She sensed that the people who wore the white coats would be looking on the streets for her. She was still mad at the daycare lady, but it wasn't the most important thing. The most important thing was to kill Arvie and rescue Jill.

Once outside the house, she looked for their car, but the driveway was empty, and so was the parking space at the edge of the street. She walked up on the porch and tried the door. Unlocked, just as she had left it. She went inside and turned on a light in the kitchen.

She was glad to see that Arvie had partially stocked the pantry and fridge. Wanda was hungry and immediately fixed herself something to eat. There were peanut butter and jelly and a loaf of bread. She loved PB & J. So did Jill. The thought didn't make her sad; it made her mad.

She went looking for a drink. There was no booze, which was disappointing but she thought she could make it at least one more day without it. It was just something else to hate Arvie for.

While she was eating, she was trying to figure out how she could get Arvie to come to the house and bring Jill with him. She would finish him once and for all and then take Jill and the car and disappear. She stared into space, her eyes focused on nothing visible to the natural eye.

Her head hurt, and all she could think of was how Arvie had become a devil. She had a list of things that he was doing wrong, but the major one was taking Jill away from her. Sometimes she wondered why she had married him to begin with. She was proud of her ability to size people up, but she had to admit, she had really missed seeing him for what he was.

The truth about him, the kind of person he really was, had come to her early in their marriage when she caught him trying to sneak the garbage out of the house. She had to put a stop to that as there was no telling what he would be taking away. She had been right too. He had taken Jill. She knew he was evil, but she never expected that. She glanced at the large knife on the counter and smiled. It wouldn't be long before she rid the earth of one Arvie Anderson.

Arvie and Jill finished their supper at a nearby cafe. Jill was full of stories about what happened at daycare, and Arvie tried his best to pay attention. But he was worried and what he worried about was distracting him from listening to Jill. What would Wanda do next? Where could he put Jill that she would be safe? Did Wanda know where Jill was anyway? He needed a plan by morning. They were back in the car when he had an idea. He turned around and headed towards their neighborhood.

Martha Smith answered the doorbell. She flashed a quick smile.

"Well, hello Arvie. What brings you and Jill over this late in the evening?"

"I've got a problem. May I talk to you for a minute?"

"Sure, come on in. Jill, Franny is in her room playing with her dolls. Why don't you go join her?"

Martha led Jill down the hall and motioned for Arvie to go into the living room. Martha soon returned, and the two of them sat down. Martha stood back up.

"I'm sorry. Can I get you something to drink? I just made some coffee. It's decaf."

Martha looked expectantly at Arvie, and he sat up straight in his chair and cleared his throat.

"No thank you. I need to explain something, and I hope you will be patient with me."

"Sure," she responded. What is this all about, she wondered.

"My wife began to drink too much and then she just went crazy. She's tried to kill me twice. I think she may have killed a telephone employee at my new house. She was locked up in a forensic unit but escaped. She tried to kill me again today. If my neighbor hadn't rescued me, she would have. She disappeared, and the police are looking for her. They just called to tell me she went to the daycare today and tried to get Jill. I'm scared to death for myself and Jill. Wanda is a very sick person, and the police can't seem to find her. I'm afraid to put Jill in a daycare facility until Wanda's caught. We're staying in a motel room at present. I can't leave her there alone. I don't have any family. I was hoping you might let her stay here tomorrow until I can find a new place for her that's safe. If not, I'll have to quit my job, and we'll have to move to another town."

"My goodness," Martha said, her hands flying to her face. "Of course you can bring her here tomorrow. You poor man. The poor child! Franny will be excited to have her here. Is there anything else I can do to help?"

"No," answered Arvie. "I just need to know that Jill is safe. I'm sure the police will find Wanda soon and get her back into custody."

"Bring Jill over here on your way to work. We'll take good care of her."

"Thanks, I'm so glad I ran into you at the park."

"Me too. How about the coffee now?"

After Arvie and Jill left, Martha shared the exciting news with Franny. Martha laughed to herself. Franny didn't know it, but she was as happy as Franny was. While Franny was getting ready for bed, Martha began to think about what she would wear the next morning when Arvie came.

Wanda lay the large knife on the counter, turned off the light and made her way into Jill's bedroom. She didn't want to sleep on Arvie's bed, and she missed Jill. In a few moments, she was sound asleep. But the sleep didn't last long. Wanda sat up straight in bed. She was sure she heard a noise in the attic above her. The house was dark, and she had no idea what time it was. She waited, sitting still but all around was silence. She lay back down and closed her eyes.

"Thump."

She heard it again. What could it be? She was certain that no one was in the house but her. Again, she waited for the sound to repeat itself. And again there was only silence. No thumps, no rustling noises, nothing. Wanda shook her head and lay back down.

She didn't close her eyes. She was afraid to go to sleep, but she was finding it hard to stay awake. By this time the moon had moved west in the sky and was beginning to shine rays into the bedroom through the double windows. Now she could make out shapes and shadows moving in the room with her.

They gave her the creeps. She decided to close her eyes and shut out the spooky shapes now showing and then disappearing in the shadows. Sleep came again and with it the noise. There was definitely something or someone in the attic.

Wanda slid the covers back and slowly eased her feet around and onto the floor. The moon was brighter now, and she could make out the attic door without any problem. She took a step towards the door and then paused. She heard a creaking sound, but it ended abruptly. She reached out to the old metal door knob. The polish was long gone, and the finish was mostly rusted. She turned it as slowly as possible hoping it wouldn't make a sound. It didn't.

The door pulled open into the bedroom, and the first landing waited in the dark for her. She stepped in and turned left towards the first riser and tread. There was a small vent in the west gable of the house, and some moonlight was making it through to spill onto the attic floor. She knew there was only the old bedroom furniture in the attic and it was on the east end of the room. Step by step she climbed the stairs toward the top of the stairway.

The walls were smooth on either side of the stairs, and she put her hands on them to steady her climb in the absence of handrails. Her head was now high enough to see across the floor of the attic. The old bedstead was just as she left it.

She stood still for a moment looking around as best she could in the faint moonlight but nothing was visible but the walls.

She took one more look and stepped up one more stair. The wood moved under her feet ever so slightly and a loud creaking sound echoed across the room. She was about to move her other foot up when something large and dark darted from her left and scurried across towards the bedstead. She screamed, threw her hands up and lost her balance.

Down the stairs she went, her head hitting the walls and the stairs over and over until she reached the landing. There her head crashed into the wooden wall that formed the landing at the bottom of the stairs.

She didn't move or make any sound. Wanda appeared to be a dead woman, but a close examination would have revealed that she was still breathing, her breath very shallow.

The night passed and at last Wanda was asleep, and no sounds woke her. The moon that had illuminated the large attic rat dropped below the horizon in the west, and the sun began climbing its way up the horizon in the east. No one knew Wanda was in Arvie and Jill's new house, not even Wanda.

The sun kept rising, throwing its warming rays on the city and soon people were waking up and moving around. Arvie got out of his bed in the motel and took a shower and shaved. He dressed for work and then woke Jill up. Once she was ready, they went downstairs and had breakfast. The motel had a nice hot breakfast, and in lieu of a kitchen in the room, it was a nice perk for the two of them. After they had eaten and had a tooth brushing contest, Arvie helped Jill pack a small rolling case with some play clothes and her favorite doll. Soon they were on their way to Franny's and Martha's.

Franny was waiting at the front door, and Jill ran up the sidewalk and stairs. Arvie heard the squeals as he was getting out of the car. Martha came out onto the front porch. She was wearing tight fitting jeans and a light blue T-shirt that showed her figure to a good advantage.

"They're really excited aren't they, Arvie?" she managed to get over the din.

"Yes, I'm glad. Maybe it'll take her mind off her mother." Arvie said.

Martha turned to look at the girls, but they were already in the house and headed for Franny's play area.

"I think she'll be alright. Have you heard anything about your wife?"

"No. I'll call the police when I get to work. I think we might have to leave town. You know, go somewhere where Wanda can't find us."

"That would make Franny sad, but you have to do what is best for the two of you." She said it but didn't mean it.

"Thanks, Martha. I'll call you if I hear something."

"Okay, try to have a nice day and relax about Jill, she'll be fine. I'll have supper for the four of us if you'll stay."

"That's asking too much. You hardly know me."

"I know enough, and I'm tired of cooking for just two."

"Okay, I appreciate it."

Arvie arrived at work a few minutes early. He wanted to talk to Melvin Shute, his big boss. Melvin's secretary was already at her desk. Arvie stopped to speak to her.

"Susan, would you please tell Mr. Shute that I need to talk to him as soon as possible. It's really important."

Susan was several years Arvie's senior and had been with the firm for a long time. She kept her finger on the pulse of the business and usually knew what was going on.

"You thinking about taking the kid and leaving town?" she asked.

"How did you know?"

"It's what most sane people would do if a crazy person was trying to kill them. Don't look shocked, it was in the paper this morning and on the late news last night."

"Oh. I've been so occupied I haven't read the paper or watched TV. I didn't want Jill to hear anything about her mother either," he said.

"I'll tell the boss. He'll help. I'm sure of it."

"Thanks, Susan, I really appreciate it." Arvie smiled politely and ended the conversation.

He moved towards his own office. He wanted to call Captain Vaughn of the police department. He set his briefcase on the floor next to his desk and sat down in his large office chair. A copy of the morning paper was lying on the top of his desk next to the computer. The story of his wife had made the headlines.

One Attempted and One Accomplished Murder

Yesterday, city police answered a call to a quiet residential area of the city. They found a telephone company employee critically wounded on the front porch of a recently rented home. The employee died later in the afternoon in spite of the heroic efforts of the EMTs and the local hospital emergency room. Mr. Arvie Anderson, the renter, was located in a neighbor's house where he had taken shelter from the assailant. According to the police reports, Mr. Anderson was attacked with a large knife twice by his estranged wife. She also is believed to have used the knife to kill the phone company employee whose name is being withheld at this time. Mrs. Anderson was already being sought by the police for injuring a nurse at the local psychiatric ward. Mrs. Anderson is considered dangerous. Anyone having information as to her whereabouts is asked to contact the local police department at once.

Arvie read the paper and then put it down with a sigh. He was still finding the whole scenario hard to believe. It was like being in a bad dream, and he thought any moment he would wake up. His phone startled him with its buzz. He answered it and then got up and walked down to Mr. Shute's office. He liked his job, and he didn't want to move, but he was scared. Afraid for himself and for Jill. If the police would just find Wanda.

Wanda woke up, dazed and sore from her fall. She looked around, and a frightening feeling came over her. Where was she? She opened the door and stepped into Jill's bedroom. She recognized the bed and bedspread. She recognized the chest and Jill's small chair. She did not recognize the room at all. She had no idea where she was or how she got there.

Wanda moved to the door and out into the dining room. She saw her furniture and in the living room area the same thing. The only thing she didn't recognize there was a recliner. What was this house and why wasn't she in her apartment? She opened the door to the bedroom. It was definitely her bedroom suite; it was not her bedroom.

She turned and walked back through the dining room and into the kitchen. A table occupied one side of the room, and her favorite placemats were at each end. A setting for two and not three. What was going on?

She turned and started towards the back door. Out of the corner of her eye, she saw a large butcher's knife laying on the counter. It was the only thing she had seen since waking up, besides the recliner, that she did not recognize. She shook her head as if to clear her thoughts. She wondered for a minute if she might be going mad.

The thought came to her that she should call Arvie and find out what was going on. She looked around the kitchen, but there was no phone on the wall or the counter. Wanda retraced her steps through the dining room and the living room. No phone on any surface or any wall. That was strange. She had always insisted there be a phone in at least two rooms.

Wanda went to the back door and opened it. She saw the grass that made up the backyard and the garage without a door. Behind the garage was another house. The backyard of the house she was in was separated from the driveway of the other house by a row of peonies. Their bright colors were dazzling in the midmorning light. She decided to walk across the yard, wade through the peonies and knock on the neighbor's door.

Wanda stood on the front porch and sighted the doorbell. The porch was neat, and there were red and white geraniums in large clay pots. She could tell the lady must be a neat housekeeper. She pushed the doorbell and waited. She heard a voice call, "Just a minute." Wanda waited patiently, and in a few seconds, the door opened wide.

Wanda barely had time to see the woman before the woman screamed and slammed the door shut. Wanda heard the lock on the door click. She just stood there not knowing what to do. She waited several minutes for her blood pressure to ease and then rang the bell again. This time there was no reply. She thought she heard voices but wasn't sure.

The voices Wanda heard was actually the voice of Mrs. Doris McClain talking to the police department on her recently repaired phone. She had trouble talking, she was so frightened, but the desk sergeant was able to walk her through it. It was just the break they had been looking for.

"Keep your door locked and don't go to the window. I've got a car on the way; you'll be safe if you stay inside."

Mrs. McClain had no intention of unlocking the door or of going outside. She called her husband who said he would come right home. Then she called Joanna. They were still talking when the first police car drove up to Mr. Anderson's house. Mrs. McClain was talking to Joanna about moving to a new neighborhood.

Wanda tried to peek in the window, but the blinds were drawn. In somewhat of a shock she managed to walk down the stairs and onto the sidewalk. Instead of going through the flowers she walked out to the main walkway and turned down the walk towards the house where she had spent the night.

Her head was hurting, and she was confused. Where was she and why was her furniture in that house and where were Arvie and Jill? It took her several minutes to make her way back onto the porch and into the house.

She left the door slightly ajar as she entered the kitchen. She thought she would look for something to eat. She discovered that she was hungry, very hungry. She couldn't remember when she had eaten last. She couldn't remember a lot of things. She knew her name was Wanda and her husband was Arvie, and their little girl was Jill. The rest seemed foggy to her.

Martha Smith was watching the two girls play. They played like they were sisters she thought. Well, if Arvie's wife got locked up maybe he would get a divorce and if he got a divorce… She dropped that thought long enough to think about what she was going to fix for supper. Her mother had told her that the way to a man's heart was through his stomach. She was a good cook, and she intended to make a meal that Arvie would remember. She also had to give some thought to what she would wear when he came over. Martha looked at her left hand where her wedding band had been. You could still see the mark of lighter skin where the rings had been.

Her first husband had been somewhat of a disappointment. The only thing good to come out of their marriage as far as she was concerned was Franny. The early years of their union had not been bad but year by year things had gotten worse. They fought all the time until Franny came. That ended the fusses for a while but when Franny was able to talk and walk she turned more and more towards her daddy. It made Martha jealous, and so the arguments began again.

Who knows what would have happened if George had not had that accident. She had warned him about using the ladder when she wasn't there to hold it, but no, he wouldn't listen to her. He never listened to her; that was the problem.

The police had investigated the accident but could find no sign of wrongdoing. His work boots had some oily substance on them, which turned out to be WD40 and they concluded that he had somehow stepped in it in the shed.

Martha had answered their questions, playing well the grieving widow but she didn't volunteer any other information. The case was closed, and she received a large settlement from the insurance company who paid double for accidental deaths. She had invested the landfall, and she and Franny lived fine off of the income and Franny's social security check.

Wanda did find some cereal, and there was milk in the fridge. She located a bowl and spoon and sat down to eat. She was facing the door when she heard footsteps on the sidewalk. She got up from the table and started towards the door. It was then she saw the knife again. It was still laying on the counter. Arvie must have left it there, and she had told him a hundred times not to leave knives out where Jill could reach them. Without thinking she picked up the knife and reached for the drawer, her back slightly turned from the door.

A uniformed police officer stepped through the door and saw Wanda with the knife.

"Put the knife down, lady."

His voice startled her. She had expected a knock on the door. She spun around to see who was in the house with her, the large knife held up in her hand. The policeman had his gun drawn as a safety measure, as did his backup who was just behind him. The policeman knew about the knife. Not only had they been briefed about "the psycho" but he had been there the day before and helped with the phone installer. He knew what Wanda was capable of with a knife.

When Wanda spun around with the knife raised, he didn't hesitate but pulled the trigger almost on instinct. The bullet hit Wanda in the chest, penetrating her heart. There was a momentary look of surprised and then she crumpled to the linoleum. She was dead when she hit the floor.

When the news was relayed to Arvie, he felt relieved and sad at the same time. He had loved Wanda and had managed to cope with her odd behavior for several years. He had hoped she would be apprehended and put in a treatment center. He didn't know for sure, but he thought if she could get treatment, maybe some kind of medicine, she would be able to function again.

He never thought about her being killed. It seemed like such a waste. Probably she couldn't help what happened to her mind. He identified her body and went to pick up Jill. Explaining the whole thing to her was going to be hard.

Four months later Arvie and Martha returned from their honeymoon. It had been a wonderful if whirlwind romance. Arvie wanted to pinch himself to see if it was real. Martha loved Jill and Jill had taken right to her. Franny was warming up to him, and the two girls were inseparable.

There were too many bad memories in the house on Chestnut and so they decided to live in Martha's house. The mortgage insurance had paid off Martha's home when her first husband had died. With Martha's investments, Franny's social security and Arvie's salary they were going to be very comfortable.

Things were really going well, and the two families were meshing together. It was almost like a dream. The dream ended on the Saturday after the honeymoon. Martha was sweeping the floor, and Arvie pulled the garbage bag out of the plastic container and tied the two red strings together. He was grabbing the back door when Martha looked up.

"What do you think you're doing?" she asked.

Arvie turned and looked at her. It was the first angry face he had seen Martha make. He just looked at her, kitchen garbage bag in his left hand, right holding onto the doorknob.

"I'm taking this smelly garbage out to the dumpster."

"Put it back!"

"Why? It smells, and I need to stretch my legs."

"Put it back and don't touch it again. I'll take it out when I'm ready to take it out. This is my house. Nothing goes out, and nothing comes in unless I say so. Do you understand me?"

Arvie's face turned white, and he dropped the bag. He went looking for Jill.

THE END

Toby's Bear

by

Philip Dampier

(Paragraphs one and twenty-five were provided by the Owl Canyon Press's Hackathon)

Beyond the cracked sidewalk, and the telephone pole with layers of flyers in a rainbow of colors, and the patch of dry brown grass stood a ten-foot high concrete block wall, caked with dozens of coats of paint. There was a small shrine at the foot of it, with burnt out candles, dead flowers, and a few soggy teddy bears. One word of graffiti filled the wall, red letters on a gold background: Rejoice!

The wet teddy bears rested side by side on the faded green bench where Charlie had sat for over twenty years weaving and selling his split oak baskets. The smallest bear sat at the end of the bench which was next to the spent flowers and the black wicked candles. The rest of the bears sat on the bench in a row from the least to the largest, proclaiming that something terrible had happened to a child. They could not talk, but their very presence indicated tragedy.

The smallest bear was dark brown with dark eyes, just like its owner, Toby. Toby's mother purchased the little brown bear three days before Toby's birth. It was the only gift, besides life, that she ever gave him. When Tobias Blackwelder went home from the hospital, the bear, two glass bottles, and a small container of baby formula accompanied him to his grandmother Maize's house.

Toby's mother left the nursery a day earlier and had not been seen or heard from for the ten years of Toby's life. In a way, that may have been a blessing because Toby was raised by a grandmother who not only showered him with love but was able to take care of him. Her husband died two years before Toby's birth; when Toby came to live with her, he filled the void the death of her husband had left.

The only other relative still available to Toby and his grandmother was his great-uncle Charlie Thompson. Charlie owned a small acreage on the edge of town, but he had long since given up his vegetable farm in favor of oak trees. The young oaks were the source of the oak strips Charlie used to make his one of a kind basket. Charlie had produced and sold the handwoven baskets for over twenty years before the teddy bears came to sit on his green bench beside the wall.

During the week, Charlie would harvest the wood which he then turned into thin strips. He then soaked the strips in water until they were soft and pliable. On Saturday, Charlie would take the strips to the city and turn them into beautiful baskets. Each Saturday, for those twenty-something years, Charlie had been sitting on the green bench next to the concrete wall weaving and waving to those who slowed down to watch.

Ladies from all over the area drove by to ooh and ah over the baskets and then place an order. The following Saturday they would pick up their basket, each one an individual work of art. Charlie's gray slacks, light blue shirt, and tan felt hat were as well-known a trademark in Southern City as his baskets.

When Charlie first began his basket weaving the concrete wall was new and covered with dazzling white paint. A shade tree grew on the other side of the wall from Charlie's bench and cast a shadow on the hot summer days. The paint on the bench was fresh and bright, making the green bench stand out against the white wall. They kept the street running parallel clean, and people waved as they passed the basket weaver.

In twenty years everything grew older, including Charlie, and with increasing age, changes occurred. The neighborhood declined, potholes multiplied in the street, and the green painted bench faded under the hot southern sun. The wall was the only part of the scene that saw renewal as young people expressed themselves with repeated coats of symbols and letters. The layers overlapped. Charlie's skin wrinkled under the same sun, and his hair turned lighter and lighter.

The baskets got better and the price Charlie received also increased. Charlie's work was in great demand, and customers considered it the height of decor to have one of his handmade oak baskets on display somewhere in your home or office. Customers still drove to the wall, but ladies were now cautious about getting out of their cars and Charlie often had to provide curb service. At the end of the day, this often meant that he had several hundred dollars in cash on his person.

Two wonderful things happened to Toby as he approached his tenth birthday. Christmas came two months before he turned ten and a Christmas Angel selected Toby's name from a tree in the mall. When Christmas morning came, the Angels presented Toby with a new bicycle. Both he and his grandmother were surprised, and Toby's world suddenly increased in size.

That same Christmas, another angel delivered a similar present to Hannah Washington, the girl who lived two doors down from Toby. Toby and Hannah were best friends and played together in the nearby public park. Now that they both had transportation, they began to explore their neighborhood together. By the time Toby's tenth birthday came, the two of them were veteran riders and pushing the envelope of their traveling territory.

Two days before Toby's birthday his great-uncle Charlie came by to visit Toby's grandmother and Toby. During the conversation, Charlie asked his grandnephew about his upcoming birthday.

"Well, Toby, now that you've got a bicycle what could you possibly want for a birthday present?"

"I want to learn how to make baskets like you do, Uncle Charlie."

"Really? It's hard work, Toby, and it's not easy to learn. Do you think you have the patience?"

"Oh, yes. I do. I want to be an artist and be famous like you."

"Well, well. Uh, Maize, do you think Toby could ride his bicycle to my bench?"

"He rides most everywhere else, him and that Hannah up the street," Maize answered.

"Okay then. You be at the green bench at 9:00 next Saturday."

Toby's birthday came and went. Maize gave him enough money to buy ice cream for him and Hannah. Toby chose the ice cream shop that was just a block from the wall and green bench. He wanted Hannah to see where he would be working. He called it working even though his uncle had not mentioned paying him. The truth was, Toby had no idea what his uncle Charlie would have him do if anything. Toby had trouble eating his ice cream before it melted because all he could talk about was making baskets and how famous he would be.

Then Saturday came. Toby was up early and put on his "work" clothes. Grandmother Maize fixed him a good breakfast and made him brush his teeth. Toby gave them a lick and a promise as he was in a hurry to get to the green bench. He wanted to get there before Uncle Charlie. That way, Uncle Charlie would know he was serious and ready to work.

Much to his surprise, not only was Uncle Charlie there, but he was already at work on a basket. Just as Toby and Hannah arrived at the wall (Oh yes, Hannah would not be left out of the excitement.) a car drove up, and Charlie set the beginnings of the basket down on the bench and eased out to the curb. Toby saw the window go down, and Uncle Charlie look in, but he couldn't hear what was being said. He did see the lady hand his uncle a sheet of paper and Uncle Charlie nod.

Toby and Hannah leaned their bikes against the graffiti-covered wall and hurried over to the bench. Toby wanted to see the basket and how his great-uncle put it together.

"Well, I only expected one student," Uncle Charlie said.

"I came to watch," Hannah said.

"You're Hannah, right?

"Yes, Sir."

"Well, this is a workplace, and I don't have time for play or foolishness. If you watch, you must be still and quiet. Can you do that?"

"Yes, Sir. I'll be quiet as a tiny mouse."

"Sit down Toby and don't talk until I'm finished talking."

"Yes, Sir."

Charlie sat down on the bench and picked up the newly started basket. It was not a particularly large bottom, but the weaving was perfect. Charlie reached down beside the bench and pulled a small strip of split oak from the pail of water where it and many more strips had been soaking. He showed the strip to Toby; then he pointed to all the strips that were standing free coming up from the woven bottom.

"This will be the first strip around the basket itself. It must be very tight against the bottom, and it must go in and out of the standing strips. Watch carefully."

And so it went for the next two months. Part by part Charlie showed Toby how to assemble a basket. Sometimes Hannah would accompany Toby, and sometimes she stayed at home to help her mother. Hannah didn't mind missing because she had absorbed all she could without taking part and the experience was growing old to her. Then on a Friday, just before the beginning of March, Toby told her his surprise.

"Guess what, Hannah. Tomorrow, Uncle Charlie is going to let me start a basket of my own. I want you to come and watch."

"I'll ask my mom and let you know in the morning. What kind of basket are you going to make?"

"Just a small one. Uncle Charlie said I could give it to you to use on Easter. What do you think of that?"

"Oh, Toby. That would be wonderful. I'm sure I can get my mom to let me go."

Hannah stood beside the bench, her eyes fastened on the small basket her friend was making. Piece by piece Toby wove the oak, making the bottom solid and tight. By lunch, he was ready to weave the sides. Charlie had brought his lunch as usual, but the two friends had to ride home for lunch. It was the fastest either had ever put a meal away. When Toby rode up to Hannah's house, she was standing by her bicycle ready to go. They were back at the green bench before Charlie could finish his cornbread and beans.

The basket weaving went on into the afternoon, with the only interruptions being two customers who came to pay Charlie for their baskets. Charlie only accepted cash and both the ladies had the correct number of bills ready. Charlie put the baskets in their cars and the money in a leather bag he used to carry his tools.

The basket handle was the hardest part, and Toby needed Charlie to help him with that part of the project. Charlie bragged on the basket, and when Toby handed it to Hannah to see, she grabbed him around the neck and hugged him. The trio was so occupied with examining the basket they did not notice the black sedan that pulled up to the curb.

Charlie turned around first and found himself staring at a dark-skinned man with a small pistol.

"What?" Charlie asked.

"Where's the money?"

Charlie pointed to the bag of tools where he had put the cash.

"Give it to me."

Charlie reached over and opened the bag. Instead of cash, he pulled out a sharp knife, the one he used to cut the strips.

166

He swung the knife, hitting the dark man in the arm. The arm jerked, and the gun went off. Charlie heard Toby cry out and Hannah scream. He turned to see Toby sliding off the bench, blood pouring from his chest. The gun fired again, and Charlie also slid down to the pavement. Hannah watched as the assailant snatched the bag and fled to the car. As soon as he shut the door, the driver took off without looking back or saying a word.

They buried Charlie and Toby at the same time side by side on Charlie's tree farm. Citizens of Southern City, who had known Charlie so well and thought of him as a town fixture, came to the funeral service and burial. It was the largest funeral in Southern City in anyone's memory. The next morning, Maize gave Hannah the small teddy bear that had been Toby's first gift requesting she take it to the wall and place it on the bench where Toby had sat to make his only basket. Before long friends filled the bench with teddy bears and the sidewalk was adorned with gifts of flowers. Many of Charlie's customers brought candles and lit them.

No one understood the shooting. Someone estimated that Charlie would only have had three or four hundred dollars or so. Why would even the most hardened criminal kill an old man and a young boy for a few hundred dollars? It didn't make sense. The candles burned until it rained and then they went out. The cut flowers died in the next day's sun while the bears sat silently, staring into the empty street.

Hannah decided that she would go to the wall the next day and retrieve the small bear. If Maize didn't want it, then she would keep it with her little basket. Hannah knew she would never forget Toby.

167

Three days later an automobile pulled up and parked beside the concrete wall. The driver opened the door but did not get out of the car. Although her face was in shadow, it was easy to tell she was sad. There was something about how she turned away from the sun and rested the weight of her hands on the steering wheel, something about her silent composure that caused Hannah to sigh. The young girl watched the driver lean out of the car and stretch her hand towards one of the burned out candles.

Then, much to Hannah's surprise, the lady stepped out of the car and picked up the small teddy bear that Hannah had come to retrieve for Maize. Hannah did not think at all but yelled out, terror in her voice.

"Stop. That's not your bear, it's Toby's bear, and I'm taking it to his grandmother."

The woman, looked up, startled. She was not aware anyone was around. She did not want to be seen nor did she did want to explain why she was taking the bear. She looked at the young girl, kissed the bear on its head and put it back where it had been sitting. Without a word or another look, she got back into her car and put it in gear. Hannah ran up to the green bench and grabbed the bear. Once she was on her bike, she peddled as fast as she could to Toby's house.

Hannah clutched the teddy bear to her chest, and once she caught her breath, the words couldn't come out fast enough.

"A lady tried to take Toby's bear, but I got it and brought it to you," Hannah said.

"What lady? What are you talking about, child?" asked Maize.

"A lady in a car. She picked up the bear, and I yelled at her, and she put it down and then she drove off, and I got the bear."

"Describe her to me, Hannah."

"She was young, like my mother. She was..."

"She was what?"

"She looked like Toby. She had Toby's face."

The woman with Toby's face drove around for a while rather than going to her motel room. She needed to think about what she was going to do. She had never meant for this to happen, never. It was obvious that her life was headed for the bottom and she felt powerless to stop it. As bad as it had been, this was even worse. She thought her past was buried and she never would have agreed to come to Southern City if she had known such a horrific event would occur.

One thing for sure, she had to find out if her fears were true or not. She had to confront RaQuen and make him tell her the truth. She had learned to ignore the voice of her conscience when she walked away from Southern City over ten years ago. Alcohol and drugs had helped, but today she was sober. She should have never agreed to come back. If she had refused, Toby would still be alive. She was certain of that.

The constant need for drugs brought them to the site of her own birth and childhood. RaQuen had connections there, a middleman supplier; all they needed was some additional cash to finish the deal. Once they had the drugs, they would go back to Birmingham and double their money. She had

169

waited in the cheap motel while RaQuen had set out in search of some cash. It never occurred to her that the cash would come from her uncle and not only result in his death but in the death of her son as well.

True, she had not seen Toby since leaving him in the hospital ten years earlier. She had not seen her uncle or her mother either, for that matter. Now, two of the three members of her family were dead, and in a way, it was her fault. She thought she could have managed it if not for the small brown teddy bear. The little bear exposed a hole in her memory. When she saw it sitting on the faded green bench, the dam of emotion broke; the experience of buying the bear for her only child came flooding into her heart. Holding his bear, even for a few seconds, completely undid her.

Toby's mother pulled into a parking place in front of the motel room. She did not shut off the car but lay across the steering wheel. Her shoulders began to shake even though she gripped the wheel harder and harder. Soon, sobs accompanied the shaking and tears came with the sobs. She felt a great sense of guilt rush over her. Guilt about leaving Toby and her mother, guilt about ignoring them both for ten years. Guilt for all she had been and done since she had left them.

Through the tears, she asked herself, "Why did I do that? Why?" She knew the answer. She was too young to be a mother, and she resented the authority figure her mother had become. She had ideas, and with the ideas there were plans, and Southern City and all that it represented was holding her back. She had to leave, get away, be herself. That's what she thought the morning after giving birth. The father wanted nothing to do with Toby, and she wondered why she should be saddled with him. Trying to raise a child

170

without a father in an African American neighborhood was hard enough but to do it as a young teenage mother would have been impossible.

I should have relied on mother to help me, she thought. I could have, but I left her to take full responsibility for Toby. That was wrong. I've known it was wrong for a long time. It was wrong to her but even worse for Toby. Why haven't I done anything about it? The sobbing stopped, and she looked at her face in the car's rearview mirror.

Her eyes cleared and the deadness she was used to seeing was replaced by a new look. Suddenly, she saw a glimmer of life. A long-forgotten spark glistened in the corner of her eyes. For the first time in years, she felt a sense of purpose rising in her heart. Her body seemed lighter, and it was as if a heavy load had been lifted from somewhere deep within.

For the first time in ten years, Maxine Blackwelder looked up and acknowledged God. "Forgive me," she prayed, but her lips did not move. Then, as if the floodgates gave way, the words came gushing forth. She bared her soul and her heart and confronted herself; when she was done with her soul-searching, she felt empty and then slowly, she began to feel full.

It was different being full of God instead of herself. A courage she had not known she possessed overcame her. She picked up her cell phone from the passenger seat and dialed 911.

"The man who killed Charles and Toby is in room 24 of the Lazy Inn motel. His name is RaQuen Walker. The room is full of drugs which he intends to sell."

"My name is Maxine Blackwelder."

"I'm outside the room, but I want to go in. I want to confront him with the truth of what he's done."

"No, Sir. I'm going in. I want him to know that he killed my uncle and my son."

"I won't tell him that you're coming, but I want to see his face when you get here."

"Yes, Sir, I'll leave the door open."

"Oh, that's easy. I've lived with him for the past five years."

Maxine opened the car door, swung her purse over her shoulder and took purposeful steps toward the door of room 24. She inserted her key in the lock and turned the handle, stepping into the edge of the room. RaQuen stuck his head out of the bathroom door and grinned.

"Time to pack up, baby. I've got the goods, and we're ready to roll. Good times are coming."

Maxine closed the door behind her but did not lock it. Her eyes took in the extra luggage on the worn carpet and then the straight razor in RaQuen's hand. She knew in the past RaQuen had used the razor for more than shaving. She stayed next to the door, semi-conscious that she might need a means of escape. Her handbag slipped off of her shoulder and into her right hand. She fixed on RaQuen's face and spoke in a low, meaningful voice.

"Those two people you killed to get the money for the drugs, they were my family. The little boy was my son.

172

You killed my son, RaQuen. I can't forgive you for that and I won't. I hope you rot in jail."

Maxine heard cars pull into the parking lot. RaQuen heard them too. He advanced towards Maxine with the razor in his hand. His face turned angry, his voice mean.

"What have you done, woman?"

Maxine turned to leave, but she wasn't fast enough. RaQuen grabbed her arm with his left hand and swung the razor in his right at the same time. Maxine screamed.

She also swung her purse which was full of cosmetics and the heavy set of keys she carried for RaQuen. The purse connected with RaQuen's arm loosening his grip just enough for her to move away from him. The movement was also away from the door and escape but temporarily out of reach of the razor. She heard car doors and voices. The cut on her cheek burned, and she felt the blood run down her face.

Maxine looked up as the door was flung open and a policeman came in but what caught her eye was RaQuen coming out of the bathroom with a pistol in his hand, the razor forgotten. She heard him fire at the officer, but then she lost consciousness. Maxine fell to the floor, her head hitting one of the drug-filled suitcases. A small pool of blood formed by her head.

Maize was surprised to see a uniformed policeman at her door. With the funeral over, she thought she was finished with the police and news people. She was still wearing the black dress she had worn when Mr. Blackwelder had passed. She had been sitting in her old rocker holding a small teddy bear in her lap. She rocked Maxine that way and then Toby. She was feeling a little sad about herself, realizing she was now alone.

Maize invited the policeman in, but he refused to take the offered seat.

"How may I help you, young man?"

"Mrs. Blackwelder, do you know a Maxine Blackwelder?"

"Yes, she's my daughter," Maize answered, the sadness suddenly replaced by a questioning look.

"We have a Maxine Blackwelder in the hospital, and she's asked us to find you."

"My Maxine?"

"Yes, Ma'am. I'm here to give you a ride if you wish to go see her."

Maize had never ridden in a police car before, but she was too emotional with her news to worry about what the neighbors might be thinking about her being carried off like that. She was trying to find out what was wrong with Maxine and why after all these years she had shown up in Southern City.

"What's wrong with my daughter that she's in the hospital here in Southern City? She lives up north of here."

"She was severely cut across her face with a razor. She's lost quite a bit of blood, and she hit her head. The doctors are just checking her out. When she came to, she asked for you and told us where you lived."

"Who cut her? What about him?"

"I don't know who he was, but he's dead. He shot an officer in the chest, and the officer's partner shot him."

"What about the officer?"

"He's stable, and we think he will be alright.

Maize walked into the emergency room where she was led to a small side room. In spite of the large bandage on the side of the patient's head, Maize recognized her daughter and found she, herself was without words. A large lump grew in her throat, choking off her breath. Her heart, which was strong, for a woman her age, skipped a beat. She stared at Maxine's eyes, knowing instantly that the pain registered there went beyond the cut on her face. She had suffered a broken heart herself, and she knew what one looked like.

Maxine tried to talk, but only tears and pitiful cries escaped her face. Maize walked to the head of the bed and leaned down until her face was next to her daughter's.

"Thank God you're alive. I couldn't stand losing you twice."

"Momma..."

"It's okay Maxine. God has forgiven you and answered my prayers at the same time."

Maize kissed Maxine's forehead gently as she had done many times in the past. Then she quietly whispered, "Thank you, Jesus."

Maxine healed. She went home with her mother and through her mother's love and tender care her soul grew stronger, and she saw good come from the bad. She found two cans of paint in the shed behind their house. She only needed two colors; those she found were red and gold. They would do just fine. With Hannah's help, she went to the wall and wrote her message behind the shrine.

In Toby's room, the bed looked clean and neat as it always did. There was a new bedspread on the bed, however, and different curtains over the windows. On the bed, its head resting on the pillow was a small dark brown teddy bear. Pictures of Toby at different ages adorned the walls. The one made at Christmas of Toby and Hannah and their new bicycles, now enlarged, stood on the nightstand. A restaurant's brown apron with a star on it hung on the back of the door.

Maxine looked in the mirror at the scar on her cheek. The wound had healed wonderfully, but the line of the razor-cut was still noticeable. It was a definite reminder of the past. It was also a sign of the present. The scar on the outside was the result of bad decisions, but the healing on the inside was the result of a mother's love and God's forgiving power. Toby's only basket, a recent gift from Hannah sat on the edge of the vanity. Maxine reached down and retrieved her hairbrush. She touched the basket's edge, for reassurance, and a long-missing smile spread across her face.

THE END

Made in the
USA
Columbia, SC